They're Only Cats . . .
Right?

Three blocks from home, I heard the first *meow*.

I sucked in a breath and glanced behind me. A black cat trotted down the center of the street.

I turned and started walking faster. My house stood two and a half blocks away.

I heard a hiss to my left. My eyes darted in that direction.

A scraggly tomcat shot across the lawn ahead of me.

I picked up my pace. The black cat behind me hissed. I started to jog.

A shiny gold Lexus sat at the corner of the next block. I shot across the street and trotted past the car.

Glancing back, I saw a pair of Siamese cats drop out of an oak tree. They landed on the roof of the Lexus. Hopped down to the pavement. And joined the black cat, the tomcat, and a striped cat.

They're following me, I realized.

They're chasing me!

FEAR STREET®
R·L·STINE

Cat

A Parachute Press Book

AN ARCHWAY PAPERBACK
Published by POCKET BOOKS
New York   London   Toronto   Sydney   Tokyo   Singapore

AN ARCHWAY PAPERBACK *Original*

An Archway Paperback published by
POCKET BOOKS, a division of Simon & Schuster Inc.
1230 Avenue of the Americas, New York, NY 10020

ISBN: 0-671-52963-3

First Archway Paperback printing May 1997

10 9 8 7 6 5 4 3 2 1

FEAR STREET is a registered trademark of Parachute Press, Inc.

AN ARCHWAY PAPERBACK and colophon are registered trademarks of Simon & Schuster Inc.

Cover art by Bill Schmidt

Printed in the U.S.A.

IL 7+

Cat

prologue

I never liked cats. Not even kittens.

For one thing, I'm allergic to them. Put me in a room with a cat, and I'll start to cough and sneeze. And my face will puff up like a marshmallow.

Also, they're too evil-looking.

Why do they have to stare like that?

What are they thinking about?

Why do they slink around so silently? As if they have some kind of guilty secret.

I know. I know.

I get carried away sometimes.

"Marty, take it easy." That's what my dad always says. "Marty, don't blow a gasket. Marty, cool your jets." Dad has a million cute expressions like those.

I admit he's right. Sometimes I forget myself. Sometimes I go too far.

Sometimes I just lose it.

I mean, that's part of being a teenager—isn't it?

But I'm telling the truth when I say I never meant to kill that cat.

That cat drove me crazy. It drove the whole basketball team crazy, living under the gym bleachers like that. Popping out when we were trying to practice. Running right over our feet.

Yeah. The cat drove us crazy.

But I never meant to kill it. And believe me, I paid for that death.

We all did.

chapter

1

On Tuesday, halfway through basketball practice, Coach Griffin lost his patience with me and the guys.

"Marty! What's your problem today?" the coach barked. "You and the other two stooges, get off my court! See if you can figure out where your passing game went!"

The ceiling of the Shadyside High gym was nearly thirty feet high and lined with white and orange lights. Bleachers stood on either side of the court— what we called schoolside and streetside.

Double doors on one end led into the school. On the other end, the scoreboard hung above the door that led into the locker rooms.

Barry, Dwayne, and I walked over to the schoolside bleachers. On the court, practice started up again.

"What's wrong with Coach?" Barry asked. "Somebody forget to tell him this is high school, not the NBA?"

Dwayne snorted. "He heard rumors he might be a nice guy. He wants to set us straight."

I laughed.

Dwayne Clark was the comedian in our group. He never took anything seriously. He and Barry Allen had been my best friends almost all my life.

"I'm serious," Barry grumbled. "Maybe we're not playing our best, but Coach didn't have to bench us."

I picked up a basketball from the bleachers and launched it at Barry's chest. He caught it easily.

Barry bounced it to Dwayne. We tossed it back and forth for a while.

Barry and Dwayne are physical opposites. Dwayne has blond hair. He is a bit on the short side for a basketball player. And he could stand to lose a few pounds.

Barry is tall, thin, and dark-haired. Some of the girls think he looks like the guy who plays Superman on television. Except for the glasses, I don't see it. When he's not playing, Barry wears black wire-rimmed glasses.

As for personality, Barry is Dwayne's opposite there too. Barry is way too serious for his own good, and he gets angry pretty easily. Too easily. Barry's hot temper often lands him in trouble.

The rest of the team thundered back and forth

across the gym. I shot the ball to Dwayne and noticed Coach Griffin glance over at us.

"Relax, guys," I said. "The coach is right. We're just not playing our best today. Maybe we need a few minutes of downtime. Friday's game is too important."

"Every game is important to you, Marty," Dwayne said. "You have a basketball scholarship to worry about."

Dwayne loved to give me a hard time about my college basketball scholarship. Getting the scholarship would make life a lot easier for me and my parents. And even though Dwayne's joking was good-natured, I thought he was a little jealous.

Barry was another story. I *knew* Barry was jealous.

"Every game is important to the Shadyside Tigers, Dwayne," I snapped. "The team is what matters to me."

"What a guy," Dwayne crowed.

And he and Barry let out hyena laughs.

If Dwayne and Barry are opposites, I am somewhere in the middle. Not too tall, not too short. Not fat, not thin. Light brown hair.

That's me. Mr. Average.

Except when it comes to basketball.

The three of us have played basketball in the circle at the end of my street since the third grade. It showed.

The Tigers were having their best year in a long time. Mainly because of Dwayne, Barry, and me. Especially because of me.

Everybody said I was the star of the team. I tried not to get a swelled head. But it wasn't easy.

We sat on the bleachers with Joe Gimmell, Kevin Hackett, and some of the other players.

Kit Morrissey was up in the bleachers too. I was surprised to see her there. I didn't think I'd ever seen her at practice before.

"Hey, Dwayne," I teased. "Kit's up there watching you, buddy. Maybe you'll get a date for the prom after all."

"She already asked me, Marty," he bragged. "I turned her down, of course. Don't want to ruin my reputation by being seen in public with her."

"Yeah, whatever," I said, waving away his lies.

Most people thought Kit Morrissey was the best-looking girl at Shadyside. But I didn't know a single guy with the guts to ask her out.

Dwayne would have a heart attack if Kit ever said hello to him.

I watched the practice for a few minutes. Coach Griffin screamed at Larry Burns again.

I picked up a small towel and wiped my face. Down the bench a bit, Kevin Hackett was fishing through a cooler.

"Anything left to drink, Hackett?" I asked.

"Only Gatorade," he replied with a shrug.

"Hey," Barry whispered, and nudged me. "Check out who just came in."

I turned to the double gym doors. Gayle Edgerton and Riki Crawford stood in front of them. Red-headed Gayle scanned the gym. She spotted me. Then she tugged on Riki's arm and walked toward us.

"Oh, man." I sighed. "I don't need this right now."

"You want to take off?" Barry asked. "I'll cover for you."

"No, man, I'm not running," I decided. "I have no reason to hide. I haven't done anything wrong."

"Okay, it's your funeral," he murmured.

Players on the court shouted and waved at Gayle and Riki as they walked along the sidelines. Kevin offered Gayle a Gatorade, but she ignored him.

Poor Kev, I thought. He'd been after Gayle for four years. She barely ever smiled at the guy.

"Hi, guys," Gayle chirped through a metal-filled smile. She is the only senior with braces. It doesn't seem to bother Gayle. She never covers her mouth when she smiles or laughs. I think it's pretty cool of her to be so confident.

"Listen, Marty," Gayle said, "I'm doing a story on the Tigers for the school paper, and I want to interview you guys. You know. About the Three Musketeers nickname. Riki is going to take pictures for the piece."

Great, I thought. That was all I needed.

Riki and I had hung out a few times. Nothing major—a movie, a pizza, a trip to the mall.

When I stopped calling her, she freaked out. She said if I wanted to break up with her, I should have just told her so instead of blowing her off.

I couldn't believe she made such a big deal of it.

"So you're going to make us stars, huh?" Dwayne joked. "About time!"

Riki looked at me expectantly. Maybe she thought I would apologize. But I didn't have anything else to say.

When Barry elbowed me, I felt instantly relieved.

"Marty—the cat!" he cried, pointing. "There it goes! *Get* it!"

chapter

2

I turned and saw the cat shoot out from under the bleachers.

The coach swore.

Dave Ionello was going for a layup. The cat zipped across his path. Dave nearly tripped over the black and silver blur. He lost his grip on the ball, which bounced away.

The cat made it safely to the other side of the gym. It ran along the bleachers on the far wall.

"Get it!" Dwayne shouted. He took off.

"Don't!" Gayle protested. "That's mean!"

Dwayne ran after the cat. It was under the basket near the double doors. When the cat saw Dwayne coming, it tore off down the sidelines.

Barry and I ran across the court to cut it off.

Coach yelled at us, but we knew he wasn't really angry.

Chasing the cat had become almost a part of practice. It had turned into a game for us.

But we never caught the cat. Somehow it always managed to get away. Coach said the cat was too fast for us.

Whatever.

"You lucked out, Marty," Barry panted, running next to me. "I think Riki wanted to pick another fight with you."

"Yeah," I agreed. "Saved by the cat."

"Get it, guys!" Dave Ionello called as Barry and I ran past him.

The coach shouted our names again. I turned and saw the smile on his face. I figured we wouldn't get in too much trouble.

The other players stopped in the middle of the court to watch Dwayne chasing the cat and Barry and me running to block its escape.

Gayle and Riki cried out for us to leave the cat alone.

"I've got it on the run!" Dwayne shouted. "Coming toward you guys!"

The cat scrambled away from Dwayne. It hadn't noticed Barry and me yet. When it did, it would probably slip under the bleachers, as usual.

As far as we could tell, it had been living under there for at least a month. I knew several kids who gave it food and water.

The cheerleaders were crazy about it and called it dumb names like Puffy and Baby.

Gayle wrote a short piece for the school paper about the cat living in the gym. I remembered reading it and smiling at Gayle's plea for someone to adopt it and give it a good home.

In a weird way, the cat became the Tigers' mascot. If it were striped, we might have made it official.

But no such luck. The cat had silvery-gray fur, and a black spot on its head shaped like a diamond.

We never really thought about what we would do if we caught the cat. The principal said an animal living in the gym presented a health hazard. So we would probably have called the Shadyside Animal Shelter.

But catching the cat wasn't the point. The chase was everything.

"Here, kitty, kitty!" Barry called. "Here, kitty."

Barry and I blocked the cat's path. It glared at us and hissed.

I reached for the cat.

It squeezed through the space under the bleachers and disappeared.

"Harper!" Coach Griffin yelled.

I spun around. I hoped he wasn't too angry. It relieved me to see that he still wore a smile on his face.

"If you're through goofing around, maybe you and the other stooges would like to play some basketball?" the coach asked.

"Excellent!" I replied.

For the second half of practice, Coach always split the team in two and played us against one another. I passed Gayle and Riki as I jogged back onto the court.

"Stooges?" Gayle asked. "I thought the coach called you guys the Three Musketeers."

"When he's happy with us, he does," I explained. "When we're not playing so well, we're Moe, Larry, and Curly."

I heard Gayle laugh as I ran out onto the court. Barry played center. He batted the ball to me at the tip-off, and we were off, down the court, toward the basket.

I passed to Dwayne, and he hit Barry in the right corner. Barry faked a three-point attempt and shot it to me inside the key. I laid it up and in.

We were back.

As I ran toward the other side of the court, I noticed Riki and Gayle chatting on the sidelines. Were they talking about me?

I hated the idea that Riki might be telling Gayle her side of the story. Especially since Gayle planned to write about me for the school paper.

Barry stole the ball, and shot it across the court at me. I almost missed the pass.

"Heads up, Harper!" Coach Griffin shouted from the sidelines.

As I ran down the court again, I glanced back at the girls. Riki was pointing in my direction. I knew for sure they were talking about me!

"Marty!" Barry shouted. "Watch where you're—"

"Whoooa!" I glanced down to see the silvery-gray cat dart in front of me.

Too late. My right foot caught the cat right under its belly.

I tried to keep my balance. But I couldn't.

I heard the cat's angry cry as I slammed into it, then tripped over it.

I fell hard to the gym floor.

Something crunched in my knee. And a burning pain shot through my leg.

With a cry of pain I collapsed to the floor.

What have I done? I wondered.

chapter

3

"Does this hurt?" the school nurse asked.

She used three fingers to apply pressure to my knee. I winced, and ground my teeth together.

"Oh, yeah," I groaned. "Could you please not do that again?"

"What do you think?" Coach Griffin asked.

"I think that cat used up eight of its nine lives today!" I growled.

"I was talking to Mrs. Nathanson, Marty," Coach Griffin snapped.

"I agree with you, Coach," Mrs. Nathanson sighed. "It's probably only a sprain. But Marty needs to rest for a couple of days, or he could do more damage. I'll give you an Ace bandage, Marty, to help keep the swelling down."

When Mrs. Nathanson had gone, Coach Griffin turned to me.

"That settles it," he announced. "Harper, I'm sorry, but you're not playing in the game on Friday."

"Aw, come on!" I cried. "You've got to be kidding!"

"Oh, man!" Dwayne groaned. "We're never going to win now. Those guys are going to eat us for breakfast."

"Coach, we need Marty," Barry pleaded.

"That stupid cat!" I snarled. "I'd better not see that animal again anytime soon."

"Listen, Harper," Coach Griffin barked, stabbing a finger toward me. "If you didn't terrorize that cat, this would never have happened."

"Oh, *please,* Coach, you know that isn't true," I groaned. "We weren't even chasing the cat when I fell. It ran out onto the court and I tripped over it."

The coach frowned at me. "If you don't want to take responsibility for hurting your knee because you were horsing around, that's your business. But winning basketball games is my business, and you're a big part of our championship plans. So take care of yourself, Marty," Coach said.

I nodded, too upset and angry to reply.

The team began to shuffle off the court. The coach followed.

Dwayne and Barry stayed with me.

Gayle and Riki watched from the sidelines. When everyone else was gone, they joined us.

"Well, this is bad news," Dwayne commented. "I'm going to wear my extra-magical Hawaiian shirt on Friday."

Dwayne had a wisecrack for every occasion, and a bad Hawaiian shirt to go with it. This year the team paid for a special game uniform to be made up for Dwayne. It was decorated with a really ugly Hawaiian print on it.

Dwayne and Barry each grabbed an arm and helped me to stand. I tested my weight on the knee.

"How is it, Marty?" Riki asked.

"It hurts," I snapped.

"Well, it's not *my* fault!" she cried.

"Sorry," I mumbled. "I'm not angry at you guys. I'm angry at that stupid cat. Anyway, my knee hurts, but I can walk."

"No way you're going to play on Friday, Marty," Barry observed.

"Yeah," I agreed sadly. "But next week I'll definitely be ready. No matter what Coach says."

"Yeah," Barry said. "You'd better be ready. Remember your scholarship."

"I don't even know if I'll get the scholarship!" I cried.

No one said anything for what seemed like a long time.

"But . . ." Dwayne began.

"I thought you told me you *already* got the scholarship," Riki said.

"I did," I sputtered. "Sort of. But it hasn't been

completely set yet. There's one other guy being considered by the university."

"How come you didn't tell us the truth?" Gayle demanded.

Then I remembered why Gayle had come to the gym in the first place.

"Gayle, this isn't for the paper," I explained. "Between us, okay?"

The last thing I wanted was for Gayle to tell the whole school I claimed to have a scholarship I didn't actually have yet.

"So, spit it out, Harper," Barry urged.

"Well, you know me," I started. "I guess I got carried away. I heard from the university that I'd made the next-to-last cut. I guess I jumped the gun."

I sighed. "I know it was stupid. But . . . once I lied, I couldn't go back and tell the truth. It would be way too embarrassing."

Nobody spoke for several seconds. Then Riki smiled and punched my shoulder. "Don't worry about it, Marty," she said. "You'll get the scholarship. I'm sure of it."

I knew Riki was only trying to be nice, but I felt better anyway. "Thanks, Riki," I replied.

I turned to the others. "Let's get out of here, guys."

"Aaaah!" I cried as I started to walk. "Wow—that hurts. I almost forgot about my stupid knee."

"Be careful, man," Barry warned. "I don't think we can win the tournament without you."

"I *know* you can't win without me," I joked.

I limped toward the double gym doors with my friends.

Then I saw it.

The silvery-gray cat stood by the doors. Even from that distance, I could see its green eyes glaring at me.

"Brave animal," Riki murmured.

"Stupid animal," I snarled. "Get it, you guys."

chapter

4

"**N**ot again!" Gayle cried.

Barry and Dwayne ran after the cat at full speed. I limped along behind them, determined to have my revenge. The cat streaked across the gym, a silver flash.

This time the cat did not run under the bleachers. Instead, it sped up the bleacher steps. Barry and Dwayne raced after it.

As I limped up the first couple of bleacher steps, Barry and Dwayne cornered the cat at the top of the bleachers. The cat darted its head back and forth, seeking an escape route.

I hurried up the steps, hating the cat more with every painful step. If it weren't for that cat, I would be in the game Friday night.

"Hey, give it up!" Gayle called. "It's only a cat. Marty, come on! You weren't even watching where you were running!"

I ignored her. When I finished with the cat, it wouldn't be hanging around the gym anymore. It would have a nice home at the Shadyside Animal Shelter.

"Here, kitty, kitty, kitty," Dwayne called.

Pain shot through my knee as I stepped onto the top bleacher next to Dwayne. Barry stood at the edge, two steps down from where the cat crouched, trapped. We weren't going to let it get away.

I moved another step, and grimaced with the pain. Stumbling up the bleachers had made it worse.

"This is all your fault, cat," I snapped.

The cat arched its back and hissed at me.

"Marty! Leave the cat alone!" Riki called from the gym floor. "Please!"

I reached for the cat, grabbed it under its front legs, and lifted it.

It hissed and squealed. The cat slashed razor-sharp claws across my hand. But I didn't let go.

The cat began to twist violently in my hands. Then its head dropped—and it sank its teeth into my forearm.

Before I could cry out, the cat ripped its claws across my forehead. I stumbled backward toward the edge of the bleachers.

Sharp pain tore through my arm and face. Blood dripped into my eyes.

"Marty, watch out!" Barry yelled.

I tried to get my footing. But my bad knee buckled. I fell toward the edge of the bleachers. If I didn't grab hold of something, I would fall.

Riki screamed.

"Marty!" Dwayne cried.

I whipped my head around, and there was Dwayne. I dropped the cat and reached out to grab his hand. Dwayne pulled me back to safety.

I turned in time to see the cat fall. It tumbled, end over end, and struck the hardwood floor at an awkward angle.

A sickening *crack* echoed through the gym.

It didn't move.

"I thought cats always landed on their feet," Barry muttered.

"So did I," I replied.

Then I heard Gayle's angry shriek. "You—you *killed* it!"

chapter
5

Gayle stared up at me. Her eyes were full of fury. "I can't believe you could be so cruel," she screamed.

"Huh?" The gym spun in front of me. I sat down on one of the benches.

"The cat!" Riki cried. "You threw the cat off the bleachers!"

The two girls stared at me, their faces white with shock.

"No!" I protested. "Come on, Riki . . . Gayle. I let go of the cat so I could grab hold of Dwayne."

"You're a total jerk, Marty," Gayle snapped. "You killed that poor cat!"

"Come on, Gayle," I pleaded. "We didn't do it on purpose. You saw—"

22

"I'll tell you what I saw!" Gayle cried. "You three morons chased that cat and threw it off the bleachers! You murdered a helpless animal, Marty. You're a . . . you're a—"

"Hey, guys," Dwayne called from the gym floor. "How about some roadkill stew?"

Barry laughed.

Gayle looked down at Dwayne. Her lips pulled back in an expression of disgust, and I thought she was going to cry.

Dwayne held the dead cat by its tail. Gayle and Riki each let out a horrified shriek. There were a few spots of blood on Dwayne's Hawaiian shirt, but he didn't seem to notice.

"Come on, Gayle," Barry groaned. "Who cares about the stupid cat? It didn't do anything but mess up basketball practice. No difference between a stray cat and a rat as far as I'm concerned."

"You idiot," Gayle sneered. "Rats are vermin. Cats are beautiful, sensitive animals."

"Well, I'm beautiful and sensitive," Dwayne announced, grinning.

Gayle's face reddened with fury. Riki stood silently, shaking her head.

"You've known me for four years," I reminded Gayle. "Do you really think I'd kill a cat on purpose? Kill any animal? Come on!"

"I know what happened, Marty," Gayle declared. "Don't try to tell me I didn't see it. I stood right here. I'm not stupid, you know."

"I never said you were! But I mean, Gayle, you

know how much I love Teddy. Killing the cat would have been like killing Teddy, my own dog. There's no way I could really hurt an animal."

Dwayne held up the cat.

"Hey, Gayle, maybe you need a fur coat?" he asked. He and Barry exploded in a fit of laughter.

"That's it. I'm out of here!" Gayle cried.

"Stop it, you guys!" I yelled. I was getting really angry. "It isn't funny."

I turned to Riki. "Help me out here, Riki," I pleaded. "You know killing an animal isn't something I would do. Yeah, I got really angry. Yeah, I chased the cat. Yeah, I wanted to get rid of it. But not by *killing* it!"

Riki ran a hand through her short-cropped blond hair.

"Riki?" I pleaded.

"I thought I knew you," she said quietly. "But I saw it too, Marty. Maybe you didn't do it on purpose. Maybe it *was* an accident. But it didn't look like an accident."

"Oh, man, you're all nuts!" I cried, and threw up my hands in surrender.

I turned to Riki again, but she wouldn't even meet my eyes.

"Okay. Fine," I sputtered. "Whatever. You and Gayle say what you want! I'm leaving! I have to get off this knee so I can play basketball next week!"

"Go," Gayle sneered. "What's stopping you?"

"I don't believe this!" I shouted. "The stupid cat

makes me wreck my knee. Then I try to get it out of the gym, and it rips into my arm and my face. I'm bleeding here, in case you didn't notice!"

I wiped blood from my forehead. Neither of the girls appeared at all sympathetic.

"Hey, I'm sorry it died, but I didn't kill it," I insisted.

Neither Gayle nor Riki spoke.

"Cat got your tongue?" Barry asked them.

"Shut up, Barry!" I yelled. "You and Dwayne are acting like idiots. Why aren't you defending me?"

Dwayne and Barry stood there, silent. At least they weren't laughing anymore.

"Well?" I urged.

"Come on, Marty." Dwayne shrugged. "Who cares about a cat?"

"Besides," Barry added, "we're your best friends. Who's going to believe us if *we* say you didn't kill the cat?"

They were right. People would be more likely to believe Gayle. After all, we were the Three Musketeers. That's what Gayle had come to do a story about.

Now the story had changed.

"Gayle, please—" I began.

"I'm through talking to you," she interrupted. "You're not the guy I thought you were, Marty. You won't get away with this."

Gayle glared at me coldly for a moment, then turned and stormed out, Riki by her side.

Dwayne and Barry hurried away. I watched them toss the dead cat into a trash can at the back of the gym.

I felt a chill. I pictured Gayle's cold stare again.

So angry. So disgusted.

Killing the cat was an accident. It was a terrible shame, I admitted. But really—what was Gayle's problem? What was the big deal?

Of course, that afternoon I had no idea just how upset Gayle was.

And I had no way of knowing that the stray cat was only the *first* death.

That others would die before the school year was over.

chapter
_____

6

I arrived at school Wednesday morning determined to talk to Gayle. Gayle had always been a good friend. Her opinion mattered to me.

I'd been so upset when I got home the night before, I couldn't even tell my parents about what had happened. We're a pretty close family, but this incident had really shaken me up.

Rain poured from the sky as I parked my mother's car in the Shadyside High School lot. I limped across the street to the front door.

A gray Saturn pulled up to the curb, and Lydia James hopped out. She covered her head with her backpack.

"Hi, Lydia," I called.

Lydia turned, noticed me, then glanced away. She jogged up the steps in front of me.

The gray Saturn pulled away with Mrs. James behind the wheel. Lydia's mother shot me a nasty look as she rolled out into the traffic.

Whoa! I thought. What did I ever do to her?

I ran up the steps after Lydia, and caught the door before it closed.

"Lydia?" I repeated. "I said hello."

She turned and nailed me with a hateful stare.

A pair of girls giggled as they passed us. Lydia hurried off toward her homeroom.

We were both late, so I didn't dare go after her. Besides, by that time I'd figured out what was going on.

Gayle.

Obviously Gayle had already talked to some of our friends. But what exactly had she told them?

That I was a cat killer?

How could any of them believe I was capable of something that cruel?

And whom would Gayle tell next? Would she write about it in the school paper?

I sighed and limped down the hall. I dodged a bunch of other students who were running late. The door to my homeroom stood open. I could hear voices from inside.

The bell rang as I slipped through the door. Most of the other students still stood around, talking.

The day didn't really begin until our homeroom teacher, Mrs. Howe, told us to sit down and be quiet.

"You're late, Marty," Mrs. Howe snapped.

I was totally taken by surprise. "I'm sorry, Mrs. Howe," I began.

"Oh, just sit down," she ordered. "You're lucky I don't give you detention."

"Detention?" I asked. "But what did I . . . ?"

"Sit down!" she snapped.

She glared at me until I trudged to my desk and sat. By then all the other kids were in their seats.

"You should be ashamed of yourself," Mrs. Howe muttered as she passed my desk.

My eyes grew wide. So *that's* what this was about! Mrs. Howe heard I'd killed that stupid cat.

Gayle had worked fast.

I glanced around the room, searching for some kind of support. Some of the guys smirked, but others seemed angry. Most of the girls frowned at me.

Great, I thought. I'll never get a date with a girl from Shadyside High again!

"Gayle has gone too far," I declared later to Dwayne and Barry in the lunchroom. "Dwayne, your little sister wouldn't even say hi to me in the hall after second period. Everyone in the school thinks I'm some kind of cat-killing psycho!"

Barry wolfed down his sandwich as if he were starving. Dwayne and I had gone for the hockey-puck hamburgers. Ketchup spotted Dwayne's orange and blue Hawaiian shirt.

"You know," Dwayne mumbled through a mouthful of burger, "this tastes a little like *cat.*"

Barry collapsed into a hacking fit of laughter.

"Come on, you guys!" I pleaded. "Give me a break. This is serious."

They tried to get themselves under control. Barry pulled off his glasses and rubbed his eyes, wiping away tears of laughter.

Dwayne tried to catch his breath. Then they glanced at each other, and that sent them into another fit of laughter.

Their floor show started to draw stares from other students, and from the ladies behind the lunch counter.

"Oh, this is really helping!" I whispered angrily.

"Okay, okay," Barry agreed. "You're right, Marty. Gayle was out of line. But what can we do about it?"

"Barry is right, man," Dwayne said. "We've both been telling everyone what really happened. But nobody seems to want to listen to the truth."

"Hey, Marty, did you know that Gayle is the president of the Animal Rights Club?" Barry asked.

"I found it out this morning," I grumbled. "She was probably the only member too. Now I'll bet she has half the school signed up."

After lunch I headed for class. I saw a group of kids gathered in front of one of the bulletin boards outside the guidance counselor's office.

I stood at the back of the group and craned my neck to see the poster that had caught everyone's attention. As I read, my stomach sank.

In big black letters, the poster read: CRUELTY TO ANIMALS! The poster announced a rally to be held the next week. I saw my name on the poster. Right above disgusting pictures of abused and tortured animals.

As I stood in shock, a girl in front of me turned. Her eyes widened when she recognized me. Quickly, she nudged the boy to her right. Before I knew what was happening, I was being stared at by at least twenty angry students.

I felt so ashamed, I said absolutely nothing to defend myself. I just turned and walked away.

How could Gayle do this to me? She had made me the most hated kid in school overnight, with one piece of distorted gossip.

Then I had a horrible thought.

"Oh, no," I gasped. "If this gets on my school record, there's no way I'm going to get that scholarship!"

I had to do something about it. But what?

Later, I found Gayle and Riki hanging out in the gym with half a dozen other girls and two guys from the track team.

"Gayle, we have to talk," I declared. "You have got to stop telling lies about me."

"Did you guys hear something?" a blond girl asked snootily.

Gayle ignored me.

"Come on, Gayle, we were friends up until yesterday," I pleaded.

"That's right, Marty," she replied coldly. "We *were* friends. Up until yesterday."

"Fine! That's how you want it?" I yelled. "You're being a real jerk, Gayle."

One of the guys, Aaron Hatcher, started to come toward me.

"Back off, Aaron," I snarled. "This isn't your problem."

"Yes, Aaron, stay out of it," Gayle agreed. "Otherwise he might do to you what he did to that cat."

"Oh, man . . ." I moaned.

Aaron grabbed my arm.

If Dwayne and Barry weren't there to drag me off, I probably would have hit him.

"Cool it, Marty," Barry whispered in my ear. "You want to get suspended? You can't afford it, and neither can the basketball team."

"Bye, Marty," Gayle sneered. "You'll be hearing more from me soon."

"I thought friends were supposed to believe friends!" I called after her.

She paid no attention.

Riki had remained silent the whole while. Now, she strode toward me.

She took my arm and led me out of the gym into the tiled hallway.

"What were you trying to do in there?" Riki demanded. "Isn't everything bad enough already without you acting like a total fool?"

"You're right. But it's all so . . ." I stammered.

"If you keep your mouth shut, maybe you can play ball again next week. You seem to be walking okay," she observed, changing the subject.

"Well, the knee is still tender," I admitted. "Coach won't let me play this week. But next week I'm in."

"If you behave," she pointed out.

"Yeah." I sighed.

People passed us on their way to class. Some stared. I'd always loved being the center of attention on the basketball court. This was different. I didn't like it at all.

"Come on, Riki. Can't you talk to Gayle for me? I know you and I aren't exactly the best of friends, but you see what she's doing to me."

"I hate to break it to you," she replied. "But I'm on Gayle's side. I think you're a sicko for what you did to that cat. I think you deserve to be punished. But I don't want the team to miss the play-offs because of you."

"I don't know what you think happened up on those bleachers," I argued. "But I never—"

Riki's sudden look of shock made me stop in the middle of my sentence. Her eyes were riveted on my face. I reached up and touched my cheek. I lowered my hand and stared at my fingers. They were wet and red.

With blood.

chapter

7

"**M**arty, you're bleeding!" Riki cried.

"Yeah, I can see that," I answered sharply. "That's where the cat scratched me yesterday. I thought the wound had closed. I must have irritated it somehow."

"I guess so," she said.

"I'll talk to you later," I told her. I took off to the boys' room without waiting for a reply.

I splashed water on my face and then dried it off with a paper towel. I grabbed a fresh towel and dabbed tenderly at my forehead.

After a minute or two, the bleeding stopped. I didn't know what I'd done to open the wound. But I was sure it would heal eventually.

As I left the boys' room, I saw Coach Griffin. He

stood inside the cafeteria door, searching for someone.

I didn't want to talk to Coach right then. I turned the other way and hurried toward my locker.

"Harper!" Coach Griffin called. He'd seen me. "Come here a minute, will you?"

Reluctantly, I turned to face him.

The coach lumbered toward me.

"Yeah, Coach?" I asked. "What's up?"

His eyes burned into mine. "I think you know what's up, Marty," he replied.

Not the coach too, I thought.

"Coach, if this is about the cat . . ."

"Yes?"

I told him my side of the story. How I started to fall and accidentally let go of the cat.

Coach Griffin glared at me. "Marty," he began sternly, "do you realize how lame that story sounds?"

"Well, yeah, I guess I do," I admitted. "But, Coach, that's what happened. I wouldn't kill an animal. You know, I've got a pet of my own."

He stared at me a moment longer, and then his expression changed.

"I believe you," he said. "Most of the teachers in the building feel the same way. Nobody wants to think you would be so cruel."

"I wouldn't, Coach," I insisted. "I swear. But I wish Mrs. Howe felt the same way you do."

"The real problem isn't the teachers," Coach Griffin told me. "The problem is the other kids. And more important, their parents."

"Huh?" I cried. "What about their parents?"

Coach frowned. "If this gets in the newspapers, it could make the school look really bad. You know. A school has to worry about its public image."

I thought about my college scholarship. I saw it flying out the window.

I suddenly felt sick.

"I'm selfish, Marty," Coach confessed. "All I care about is my basketball team. All I care about is winning the championship. And any bad newspaper stories are going to be very bad for the team."

He frowned. "The rumors are that you actually killed the cat. And that Dwayne and Barry helped you."

"What are you saying, Coach?" I asked nervously. "You want me off the team?"

His frown deepened. "No, Marty. I want you back on the team as soon as possible. Problem with that is, the Animal Rights Club is making a big thing out of this. If you want to play in next week's game, well . . ."

"What, Coach?" I pushed. "What do you want me to do? I'll do whatever I have to."

"The principal asked me to speak to you. He wants you to face the club's charges in Student Court tomorrow."

"But that isn't right!" I protested. "The Student

Court kids are all Gayle's buddies. If I go on trial there, they're going to eat me alive!"

"They'll be fair," Coach replied softly.

But I knew they wouldn't be. I knew I was doomed.

chapter

8

Student Court met in the gym the next day during lunch period.

The maintenance crew brought in a teacher's desk for the judge. It stood under the far basket, facing the bleachers.

Next to that stood a wooden chair used as a witness stand.

I sat in a similar chair, facing the judge's desk. Everyone else sat on the bleachers.

A lot of students and teachers were there. I searched the faces and breathed a sigh of relief when I saw that my parents weren't there.

Last night I'd told them the whole story. They were very understanding.

They offered to attend the Student Court today and show their support for me.

I felt grateful. But I told them I could handle it myself.

But could I?

Sitting there in front of everyone, I couldn't believe how nervous I felt. My hands were cold as ice. My mouth felt so dry, I kept swallowing.

I wondered if everyone could see how tense I was.

I crossed my legs. Tried to appear calm.

After all, I knew I was innocent.

But what would the Student Court decide? And if they found me guilty, what would my punishment be?

Riki was called up first. She seemed nervous too. But she told her version of the story simply.

Dwayne and Barry followed. They did surprisingly well. Dwayne didn't try to be funny. And Barry told everyone about how much I loved my dog, and how I'd never hurt any animal.

I'd always considered Student Court to be a goof. But suddenly I had to take it very seriously.

My reputation and college career depended on it.

Next, Mrs. Howe asked Gayle to come forward. I stopped listening. At least, I tried to. But after a minute, I couldn't help it.

". . . he grabbed it, and he threw it over the side of the bleachers," Gayle was saying. "Then, he and Dwayne and Barry swung it around, teasing us. Then, I left."

"That's not true!" I shouted, jumping up from my seat. My voice cracked. A couple of kids laughed.

"Sit down, Martin," Mrs. Howe ordered.

"But I—"

"Martin. Sit down. You'll have your turn."

I sat down.

Finally, I got to tell my side of the story. I was questioned by a girl named Jessica Wells. She was acting as the lawyer for the Animal Rights Club. I had a lawyer too. He would have the chance to ask me questions when Jessica was through.

"So, Marty, you claim that you did not tease Gayle with the dead cat. And you didn't throw it in the garbage?" Jessica asked, trying to sound like a real lawyer.

"Absolutely," I declared. "You've already heard the same story from Barry and Dwayne. Even from Riki! I never touched it after . . ."

"After what?" Jessica demanded. "When did you last touch the cat?"

"Well, when I dropped it," I said.

"When you dropped it?" Jessica asked loudly. "I see. Let me ask you one more question."

"Okay," I murmured.

"Did you tell your friends you were going to 'get rid' of the cat?" Jessica asked.

The auditorium filled with whispers and gasps.

"Well, yes. Yes. I guess I said that. But . . . but what I meant was . . ."

No one was listening now. Everyone was talking and whispering.

The jury stayed outside the gym for fifteen minutes. When they filed back into the room, several of them wouldn't even look at me.

They surprised me though.

"The jury finds the defendant, Martin A. Harper, *not guilty* of the murder of the cat," Carey Donovan read.

I heard groans and gasps of surprise from the bleachers. A couple of kids applauded.

I let out a long sigh of relief.

"However, in the matter of cruelty to animals, the jury finds you *totally* guilty," Carey continued reading.

Then she glanced up at me. "Jerk."

"Hey!" I protested.

"That's enough, Carey," Mrs. Howe scolded. "Thank you. Thank you all for taking this seriously and doing such a responsible job."

Mrs. Howe leaned over the desk. "Martin, since you have been found guilty of cruelty, you will have to serve thirty hours of community service at the Shady-side Animal Shelter. Your sentence will begin this week."

Thirty hours?

With studying and basketball, I wouldn't have a spare minute for weeks!

I started to protest. But then I saw something move under the bleachers.

I saw a shadow shift.

A dark form slithered out from under the seats.

Green eyes glared at me from either side of a black diamond spot.

"Oh, nooo," I moaned.

It was the cat. The silvery-gray cat.

chapter

9

"It—it's there!" I choked out.

I pointed to the glowing green eyes under the seats. "The cat—it's alive!"

I jumped up. My legs trembled as I darted toward the bleachers.

Several other kids leapt to their feet. They began peering under the seats.

I heard a lot of laughter. A lot of confused voices.

"There's no cat there!" someone reported.

"Were you looking at this?" a girl asked. She picked up a high-top sneaker from under her seat.

"It was there!" I insisted, still pointing at the spot. "It really was!"

"Enough, Marty," Mrs. Howe cried. "Just stop it. This isn't funny."

"You're right about that," I agreed. "There's nothing funny about any of this."

That afternoon I brought my history book to practice. I sat on the sidelines, reading my assignment.

Finals weren't that far away. I figured I might as well get a head start.

As usual, there were several girls behind me on the bleachers, watching practice. One of them was Jessica Wells.

She climbed down and sat next to me. She was majorly cute, with bright, shining green eyes, a great smile, and long, straight brown hair.

"Hey."

"Hey."

"I wanted to say I'm sorry," she began. "Being a lawyer in Student Court is something you have to do for social studies class. It was my turn. I didn't want to get you into any trouble."

"Wow," I replied. "Thanks a lot. Most people wouldn't be caught dead even talking to me right now. Since I'm a big, bad cat killer."

She frowned. "I'm glad they found you innocent of that part."

The Tigers pounded back and forth across the court. But staring into Jessica's green eyes, I barely remembered they were there.

"Yo, Harper!" Dwayne cried. When I turned to the court, he and Barry both gave me the thumbs-up.

I laughed, and so did Jessica. That was good.

Then I noticed Riki.

She stood by the open double doors of the gym, glaring at me and Jessica.

"Hey!" I called to Riki. I smiled and waved her over, as I would any other friend.

"Hi, Riki!" Jessica called.

Riki spun and marched out of the gym. Her back was stiff with anger.

"What's her problem?" Jessica asked.

I didn't really want to get into it. But I thought no answer would be worse than half of one.

"We went out a couple of times," I admitted. "She doesn't know why I stopped calling her."

"Why did you?" Jessica asked.

The question caught me off guard. "I don't know," I finally replied. "I guess I just didn't want to get serious with her, or anything."

Jessica and I sat and watched basketball practice together in silence. The team played well. I thought they might actually be able to win without me the next night.

When her friends came down the bleachers and headed for the doors, Jessica stood up. "Well, my friends are leaving. I'd better go." She sighed.

I said good-bye and thanked her for the kind words. Then I picked up my textbook and settled into my reading.

A few minutes later I heard a small cry.

When I heard it again, I knew it was a meow.

chapter

10

With a startled cry, I leapt up onto the seat.

"Mmreowr! Hissssss!"

I turned—and saw three girls about a dozen steps above me.

They were laughing.

Had they made the cat sounds?

Why was everyone being so cruel?

After practice, Coach Griffin approached me.

"You should have been paying more attention to practice, Marty," he scolded. "I wanted your feedback on how to cover for your absence."

"That's easy, Coach," I answered. "Move Lenny to

center and let Dwayne and Barry both play forward. The guards are fine where they are."

Coach Griffin smiled. "So, you paid attention after all."

"Some," I answered.

"Listen, Marty, I want you to know you did the right thing today, standing up for yourself. The Student Court made an example of you."

He shook his head. "I don't think that's fair. I'm going to try to get your sentence lightened. We need you rested up for your return to the game next Friday."

"I'll be okay, Coach," I promised. "Besides, I've been thinking about it. I didn't kill that cat, but maybe I was a little cruel to it. I should take the punishment and serve the full thirty hours."

Coach's eyes widened with surprise.

"You're a good kid, Marty," he whispered. "But if you tell anyone I said that, I'll make practice your personal torture session every day until the season's over."

I grinned. "Thanks, Coach."

That night after dinner, I studied history until well after ten o'clock. Teddy, my Chinese shar-pei, slept soundly on my bed. Every once in a while he would lift his head and shake his velvety, wrinkled body.

When history didn't make sense to me anymore, I tried trigonometry.

Every few minutes I thought about the past three

days. About Jessica Wells, and Coach Griffin's comments.

I also thought a lot about Gayle and Riki, and about the poor, stupid cat.

And I thought about seeing that cat under the bleachers during Student Court. And about hearing the yowling and hissing while the team practiced.

Was I seeing and hearing things?

Were kids playing a cruel joke on me?

The phone rang, startling me. I glanced at the clock as I lifted the receiver. It read eleven-fifteen.

"Hello?"

Silence.

"Who is this?" I demanded.

Then, I heard someone breathing. Not heavily, the way most prank phone callers do. Softly.

"Hello? Who *is* this?" I demanded again.

I slammed the receiver down.

My heart beat loudly in my ears.

The phone rang again.

I stared at it.

The phone rang again.

I swallowed hard.

On the third ring, I picked it up.

"You're going to pay, Marty," a gruff female voice whispered. "Do you hear me? You're going to pay for what you did!"

"Hey—who is this?" I cried.

And then I recognized the voice.

chapter

11

"**W**hat's your problem, Riki?" I asked furiously.

"What's *your* problem?" Riki shot back.

"For the *last* time, I didn't kill that cat!" I declared.

"I'm not calling about the cat!" Riki growled. "I know what you did, you jerk!"

I flopped down on my bed, next to Teddy. With a sigh, I stared out the window.

"I want to go to sleep, Riki. Why don't you just tell me why you're screaming at me in the middle of the night. Then we can both hang up and I can get some rest."

Clouds drifted across the moon. I sank back on the pillow and stared up at the sky.

"Well, Riki?" I repeated.

49

"You sat there flirting with Jessica Wells. And then you waved to me as if everything were fine!"

"Oh, man."

I sighed and closed my eyes in frustration. "Why do you care who I talk to? For the last time, I'm not your boyfriend, Riki. Besides, I thought you hated me now. You know, for killing the cat."

"Jessica is only the latest insult," she snarled. "I hear you're interested in Kit Morrissey too."

"Please," I moaned. "What guy at Shadyside isn't interested in Kit?"

"And," Riki continued, "Gayle told me today that she saw you out with Lisa Greene the night you canceled a date with me. You said you were sick."

She groaned. "You're such a liar, Marty. I can't stand to be lied to."

What could I say?

Riki was right. Still, I had to say something to get her off the phone.

"You know what, Riki?" I said. "You're right. I went out with Lisa instead of you that night. We didn't have a good time, but you don't care about that. I lied to you because I thought it would be better than hurting your feelings."

I took a breath. "Maybe I shouldn't have cared about your feelings," I continued. "But I hoped we could be friends. I guess I was wrong."

"Were you ever!" she shouted so loudly, I pulled the phone away from my ear.

"Oh, you're such a sensitive guy, Marty, not wanting to hurt my feelings," she shrieked. "If you didn't want to hurt my feelings, you shouldn't have lied to me in the first place! I hate you. I really do!"

"Get a life, Riki," I replied.

She slammed down the receiver.

I stared up at the sky, letting the dial tone hum in my ears.

In school the next day, I minded my own business. I had no more interest in arguing with anyone about the dead cat.

Most kids acted as if nothing had happened. Life pretty much returned to normal.

By the end of the day I felt much better. My sore knee still throbbed, but my mood was good. Maybe the whole awful thing was behind me.

After supper, my dad dropped me off behind the school for the basketball game. I hobbled through the back entrance into the locker room.

Coach Griffin called a hello.

I stood by the door that led into the gym and listened as he gave his usual pep talk. As the team jogged past me, a lot of the guys patted my shoulder or flashed me a thumbs-up.

The crowd cheered when we entered the gym. But another sound soon joined the noise.

It was meowing. The other team was mocking me.

I felt sick with embarrassment and anger.

I hung my head and wished I could be anywhere but in that gym.

Dwayne shouted at them to shut up. Barry, Kevin, and some of the other guys started to yell also.

But the other team didn't stop until Coach Griffin stalked across the court and whispered something to their coach.

Soon after that, the meowing stopped.

As the game began, I heard more meowing from the bleachers. I tried to ignore it and concentrate on the game.

But it wasn't easy.

At halftime, a gentle hand touched my shoulder.

"You okay?" Jessica Wells asked.

"I'll be all right." I sighed. "I wish I knew who is still spreading the word about the cat."

She shrugged. "Probably Gayle, don't you think?"

"Who else?" I replied.

"You know," she said, "I don't think they're making fun of you because you killed that cat."

"What other reason is there?" I demanded.

"I think they're making fun of you because you kind of freaked at the Student Court. You know, when you said you saw the cat."

"I *did* see the cat," I insisted.

Jessica stared at me intently.

"I don't know if it was the same cat," I added. "But it *looked* like the same cat. I don't know. I just want this stupid cat thing to go away."

"It will, Marty," she promised. "Gayle and the Animal Rights Club have organized a rally against cruelty to animals. But once that's over . . . Just give it time."

"Yeah. Time," I muttered.

"So," she said, her voice light, "I hear you're going out with Lisa Greene."

I smiled.

"Something funny?" she asked.

"Sort of," I admitted. "The way rumors fly around this school."

"So, you're not going out with Lisa?"

"We went out once," I replied. "But that's the whole story. We're just friends."

Jessica grinned. "Good."

We smiled at each other. Then we both lowered our eyes.

I kept smiling though. People could tease me all they wanted as long as girls like Jessica kept smiling at me.

I didn't get home until nearly ten. I wanted to fall into bed and not open my eyes until morning. But I knew I wouldn't get much studying done during the next two nights at the animal shelter.

I sat at my desk. I cracked open my math book and began to read.

"Huh?"

I jumped up when I heard cats screaming.

Now fully awake, I crawled across my bed to the window and peered out.

I could not see them, but somewhere out in the darkness, two cats were fighting. Their cries were horrible—and very close to the house.

Kneeling on the bed, I shut the window.

It didn't help.

I could still hear their fight, still hear them yowling and hissing at each other.

Finally, I heard a deafening shriek.

Then silence.

"Whoa." I let out a sigh.

Then I sank back into my desk chair and opened my history book. But I felt too tired to concentrate.

On my third yawn, I decided to call it a night. I closed the history book and stretched.

Something scratched at the window over my bed.

I jumped up from the desk, knocking the chair to the floor.

I stared at the window.

Nothing there.

Then I heard more scratching. Claws against glass.

My heart hammered in my chest.

I heard a soft hiss.

Then more clawing at the window.

Whatever was outside wanted to get in.

chapter

12

"*H*ey!" I cried out. Something clattered against the glass.

A stick?

Then a handful of pebbles clicked off the window.

"Man, I'm going nuts!" I muttered.

It wasn't a cat clawing at the window.

I peered out at the yard. Dwayne and Barry stood under the large oak tree. They were waving for me to join them.

I hobbled over to my closet and pulled on a navy blue sweatshirt. Then I crawled across my bed and slid the window open.

I reached out for the tree, grabbed hold of a thick limb with both hands, and pulled my legs behind me. I'd performed that trick dozens of times, but never with a sore knee. Pain shot up my leg. I nearly lost my grip and fell into the shrubs below.

Ignoring the pain, I shimmied down the branch and slid down the trunk to the ground.

"Hey—nice outfit!" I told Dwayne.

"What?" he protested. He stared down at the purple and green Hawaiian shirt he wore. "You mean this? What's wrong with this?"

"Well," I replied, "I like it better than the blue one with the pink flamingos."

"That's not a Hawaiian shirt," Barry added. "It's a white shirt. Someone threw up on him."

Barry and I laughed.

"So, where to?" I asked.

"The Corner," Barry replied. "Where else?"

The Corner is a popular Shadyside hangout about a block from school.

We all hung out at The Corner a lot. And when I didn't know where to take a girl on a date, we'd wind up there.

We stood in line to order, then slid into a booth at the back of the restaurant. We could see everyone who came in. If anybody we knew showed up—particularly girls—we wouldn't miss them.

"So, Marty," Barry said with a mouthful of pizza, "what happened yesterday in Student Court? I mean, you lost it."

I froze. "What do you mean?"

"You know. Seeing the cat."

I didn't answer him.

"The cat, Marty. The cat. Hello? You said you saw the dead cat under the bleachers," he reminded me.

But I didn't need reminding. I gazed at Dwayne, but he wouldn't meet my eyes.

"I *did* see that cat," I insisted. "I know what I saw. It sat there and stared at me."

Barry and Dwayne looked stunned.

"Kind of the way you're staring at me now," I added sarcastically.

"Whoa!" Barry exclaimed. "Wait a minute. You really believe you saw the same cat we all watched fall off those bleachers and die? The same cat Dwayne and I threw in the garbage?"

"That's right," I replied.

I knew it sounded nuts. But these two guys were my best friends. If I couldn't tell them the truth, who could I tell?

"Aw, come on!" Barry cried. "You've got to be kidding me!"

"I saw the cat," I repeated. "Maybe it's not as dead as we thought. Or maybe there was more than one cat living in the gym."

They both stared at me. And didn't say a word.

Later, we hurried toward my house. If my mother checked in on me after eleven and didn't find me in my room, I would be in big trouble.

My knee felt okay. But no way could I climb back up the tree and into my room. I had to go through the front door. I only hoped my parents were asleep.

A block before my street, I turned left.

"Where are you going?" Dwayne asked. "Can't find your own house in the dark?"

"We'll cut through the backyards," I explained. "It'll be quicker."

I headed for the Millens' house. A stretch of woods separated their backyard from mine. The three of us moved silently up the Millens' driveway. Their house was dark. The night seemed to swallow us up.

"Spooky," Dwayne whispered.

I heard crickets. Wind rustled the leaves over our heads. We walked along the side of the house. I noticed that the side door hung open behind the glass storm door.

As we passed the door, I saw a shape in the darkness beyond the glass. Something watched us.

"Hey, guys . . ." I whispered.

Something slammed against the inside of the storm door. We cried out in surprise. I tensed to run as a snarling dog threw itself against the door again.

"Whoa!" Dwayne cried. "I'm too young for a heart attack."

We hurried through the backyard. And reached the narrow path that cut through the small stretch of woods, connecting my yard with theirs.

"Through here," I told my friends, and we slipped into the woods.

A few feet along the path, I could see my house through the trees. The downstairs lights were on, but my bedroom was still dark. I hoped my parents didn't even know I'd gone out.

I heard a loud hiss above my head.

"Hey!" Dwayne shouted.

I heard the screech of an animal. From a tree branch above us.

Then a *thud*.

Something landed heavily on Barry's head.

"Help me!" he gasped.

chapter

13

"Get it off me!" he screamed. "Get it off!"

A cat!

Barry desperately wrestled with it. But it hung on to his head with its claws.

Dwayne picked up a big branch and swung it over his shoulder.

"Stop!" I cried. "You'll hit Barry."

Dwayne dropped the branch.

I dove at Barry. Grabbed the cat with both hands. And pulled it off his head.

I dropped the screeching cat on the ground.

Dwayne stuck a foot under its belly and kicked it deep into the woods. I heard it crash through branches and bushes, howling all the way.

"Oh, wow," Barry moaned. "Oh, wow."

"Barry, let me see your face," I said.

I squinted through the darkness. His cheeks were scratched. But nothing too deep.

"You're okay," I told him. "But someone should look at those scratches."

"Was that it, Marty?" he asked. "Was that the cat?"

"No way, man," Dwayne chimed in. "That other cat is dead, remember?"

I remembered, all right. But as dark as the woods were, I had a good look at the cat that attacked Barry. I was pretty sure I'd seen a black diamond on its forehead.

"Marty?" Barry asked.

"No," I replied firmly. "That cat is dead, Barry. That cat is dead."

The next night, Saturday, I started my community service at the Shadyside Animal Shelter. A one-story square building, the shelter offered help to all kinds of animals. But most of their customers were stray cats and dogs.

The manager, Carolyn Peters, seemed really nice. I asked what my duties were. She told me she wanted me to sweep the floor, feed the animals, and call her at home if any of them appeared to be sick.

A breeze.

Most nights, they needed me at the shelter by seven o'clock, when Carolyn left for the night. Between nine and eleven, a night watchman came on, and I was free to go home.

That first night, I started with the sweeping. After a while, I entered the kennel area. Leaning my broom against the wall, I crouched down to look at the animals.

On the left, dogs snoozed in two long rows of cages stacked two high. On the right, cats prowled in the same setup. A few of the cages housed more than one animal.

A yellow-eyed, gray tomcat stared at me from a bottom cage. Without warning, it hissed and arched its back.

"Yeah? The same to you, buddy," I muttered.

I thought about what had happened to Barry the night before, and a shiver ran through me. I didn't want to be around cats any more than I absolutely had to be. At nine o'clock I'd feed them. After that, I would settle in the small office and study.

That way I wouldn't have to spend much time with the cats, and my allergies wouldn't act up.

I picked up the broom and turned to leave the kennel.

But a sharp *thud* made me spin around.

"Who's there?" I demanded. "Is someone back there?"

No reply.

I saw a small light flash across the dark room.

Then, the animals came alive.

The dogs began to bark and howl. The cats began to hiss and screech.

I clapped my hands over my ears, trying to block out the terrifying noise.

"Stop it!" I screamed. "Stop it!"

The animals heaved themselves against their cages. The hissing and shrieking grew louder. Louder.

"Stop it!" I screamed. "Stop it! *What's going on?*"

chapter 14

"Stop it! *Stop it!"* I shrieked.

I pressed my hands tighter against my ears. But I couldn't shut out the sound of their cries.

Cats clawed at their cages. Screeching. Hissing. Their mouths pulled back in fierce sneers. Their eyes flashing and wild.

Dogs tossed back their heads and howled.

"Please!" I begged, my heart pounding.

Holding my ears, I turned and ran from the room. I slammed the office door behind me. But I couldn't shut out the noise.

I dove for the desk. Grabbed the phone in a trembling hand. And punched in Carolyn's number.

"Come quick!" I managed to choke out. "Please. Hurry! Something is wrong! Something is terribly wrong!"

"But, Marty—" she protested. "I just got home. What's happening?"

"Just come," I pleaded. "Hurry."

I waited in the office until she arrived. The screeching and barking didn't let up. I could hear dogs banging against their cages. And over it all, the shrill hiss of cats.

About ten minutes later, I saw headlights in the office window. Carolyn's car rolled into the parking lot.

Holding my ears, I ran to the front door. I unbolted it and pulled it open.

The hissing and screeching stopped.

"Huh?" I let out a sharp gasp.

Silence now.

Carolyn stepped up to the front door. Her eyes anxiously swept over the cages. "Marty—what's wrong?" she demanded.

In the lunchroom on Monday, I told the story to Barry and Dwayne.

Barry shook his head. Dwayne let out a long whistle. "Weird," he murmured.

"Did the shelter manager believe you?" Barry asked.

I shrugged. "I don't know. She just stared at me." I sighed and shoved my sandwich away. "I don't know *what* to believe anymore."

"Hey, cheer up," Dwayne urged. "It could be a lot worse, Marty."

"Worse?" I replied. "How?"

He thought about it. "I don't know," he said finally.

We all laughed. But my laughter was forced.

On my way out I was thinking about cats and dogs—and bumped right into someone.

"Oh, sorry," I mumbled.

It was Kit Morrissey.

"Hi, Marty," she said, and gave me a big smile. "What's up?"

For a few seconds I couldn't say anything. Kit had moved to Shadyside during the December break. She had quickly become one of the most popular girls in school.

Her chestnut-brown hair fell to her shoulders and perfectly framed her face. Her eyes were emerald green, swirled with flecks of gold.

"Um," I fumbled, "you were out a couple of days, huh?"

"I was sick. The flu or something," Kit reported. "I feel fine now."

"You *look* fine too," I flirted.

"You're not so bad yourself, Harper," she replied.

"Uh, you want to grab an ice cream or something at The Corner after school?" I asked.

Her eyes narrowed. "Don't you have practice?"

"I messed up my knee last week," I explained. "I can't really practice. If I miss one day of watching, Coach won't completely freak."

Kit tilted her head thoughtfully, then nodded.

* * *

CAT

I met Kit on the side steps of the school, and we walked to The Corner. We talked for almost two hours. She was really cool. I was falling for her, hard.

As we were leaving The Corner, something made me glance back inside. When I did, I froze.

In the back, Riki sat at a booth by herself. She was glaring at me. I didn't know how long she'd been sitting there. I didn't really care either. Forget it, I thought. Forget her.

I turned away and let the door slam behind me.

Kit lived on Canyon Road. We strolled down the tree-lined street, chatting comfortably, as if we'd always been friends.

Cars whizzed by. Several people beeped at us, but I didn't even turn to see who was trying to get our attention.

I was feeling very happy. Something really great was happening between Kit and me.

We turned up her driveway. She lived in an old brick house with ivy growing across the front wall.

"Do you want to come in for a while?" Kit asked. "Or do you have to get home for dinner?"

"Not right away," I answered happily.

Kit unlocked the door and stepped inside. "What are you waiting for?"

I followed her in. She closed the door behind me. I glanced around the front hall. Stairs led to the second floor. A long hallway led to the kitchen. To the left, an arched passage gave way to the living room.

"Nice house," I commented.

And then I jumped as a black cat came running down the stairs toward us. I heard a *meow* to my left.

A striped cat darted in from the living room. Two white kittens with spiky fur trotted down the hall from the kitchen.

A few feet up ahead, a gray cat sat on its haunches and glared at me.

I opened my mouth to say something.

But before I could speak, the cats all arched their backs and opened their mouths in a shrill, terrifying hiss.

chapter

15

"Get them away from me!" I wailed.

Kit laughed. "Marty—relax. They're just hungry."

I could feel my face turn red.

My legs were shaking. I hoped Kit couldn't see how really scared I was.

"Uh . . . after the thing with the cat at school, I guess I'm a little messed up," I admitted.

"I heard about that," Kit said. She had to shout because the cats were still hissing. "It was an accident—right?"

"Yeah," I replied uncomfortably.

Kit tossed her backpack to the floor. "Want to hang out awhile? Maybe the cats will all calm down once they get to know you."

She didn't want me to leave. I couldn't believe it! Kit actually liked me.

If only we weren't surrounded by those annoying, hissing cats.

"How many cats do you have?" I asked.

She grinned. "A few."

My eyes swept around the room. Cats were perched everywhere I looked.

"I—I've really got to go," I stammered. "If I don't ace my math test . . ."

Kit looked hurt.

I felt bad. But those cats—they were really giving me the creeps.

And I'm so allergic to them. I could already feel my nose clog up and my face start to puff.

"Later," I said, moving to the door. "I'll call you or something. Okay?"

The black cat brushed against my leg. It arched its back stiffly as it moved past me.

A plump white cat with a very long tail let out an angry screech from the stairs.

"I—I guess I'd better feed them," Kit said, shaking her head. "It's so odd, Marty. I don't understand it. They've never acted like this before."

"I—I just have a way with cats," I joked.

And then I ran out of there as fast as I could.

"Are you sure this is a good idea?" Barry whispered. "We could get in major trouble."

"Give me a break," Dwayne snapped. "This is

going to go down in history as the greatest gag ever pulled at Shadyside High School."

"Marty?" Barry asked, waiting for my opinion.

"We've got to do it," I answered. "Gayle deserves it, man. She still won't let it drop. When she sees us, she acts as if we don't exist. That article in the school paper about my Student Court trial was the last straw."

We were supposed to be in the locker room getting ready for practice. But Dwayne's brainstorm needed to be acted upon right away. The Animal Rights Club met in a first-floor classroom after school every Tuesday.

"It's time to teach Gayle a lesson," I whispered.

Barry still appeared to be worried.

"Come on, Barry," Dwayne urged. "Marty took all the heat for the cat incident. We've got to make it up to him somehow, right?"

Barry nodded. "Right."

I stood outside the closed door of the classroom in which the Animal Rights Club gathered. I could hear Gayle droning on inside. At one point, I heard her mention my name. Any doubts I felt about what we were doing totally disappeared.

I checked my watch. Seven minutes past three. Barry and Dwayne would be at the open window by now. Any second now, I thought.

Then the screaming started.

I heard shrieks and startled cries.

"Get them out of here!" a girl cried. "Get them away from me!"

"Rats!" a boy shouted. "Hundreds of them!"

No kidding, I thought. A grin spread across my face.

Barry, Dwayne, and I had stolen a dozen white rats from the biology lab and placed them in a box. At seven past three, Dwayne dumped them through the classroom window where the Animal Rights Club met.

The door banged open and the club members started to pour out into the hallway. I saw a couple of rats scurry past me and down the hall. I moved to the open doorway. Gayle and two other girls were chasing after the rats.

"Get them out of here!" Gayle cried.

At that moment, she saw me. "Did you have anything to do with this?"

"Of course not," I replied. But I couldn't keep a straight face.

I heard laughter from outside the window. Dwayne and Barry.

Gayle shot a nasty glance their way. The guys ducked. But Gayle ran over to the window.

"I see you!" she screamed. "I see you, you jerks! You're in major trouble!"

"And so are you!" she barked at me.

"Me?" I asked innocently. "What did I do?"

"I'm going to get you for this, Marty," Gayle snarled. "This isn't over. Not by a long shot."

"Yes, it is," I answered. "Yes, it is."

* * *

I told Kit the story at The Corner later. She laughed until tears rolled down her face.

"That wasn't too nice," she scolded. "But it was pretty funny."

The embarrassing scene at her house with the cats the day before had become history. She promised to help me with math, and I asked her to go to the movies on Saturday night.

She said yes.

Then she kissed me! Because we were sitting in a booth at The Corner, it was a quick kiss.

For a second I thought about Jessica, who had waved to me in the hallway that morning. Then all thoughts of Jessica were gone. Kit Morrissey was the only girl I could think about.

Later, when I walked her home, she didn't ask me to come in. Maybe she didn't want a repeat of the previous afternoon.

Well, neither did I.

Humming to myself, I turned off Canyon Drive and headed for home. When I reached Fear Street, clouds covered the sun. The air grew cool.

Three blocks from home, I heard the first *meow*.

I sucked in a breath and glanced behind me. A black cat trotted down the center of the street.

I turned and started walking faster. My house stood two and a half blocks away.

I heard a *hiss* to my left. My eyes darted in that direction.

A scraggly tomcat shot across the lawn ahead of me.

73

I picked up my pace. The black cat behind me hissed. I started to jog.

A shiny gold Lexus sat at the corner of the next block. I shot across the street and trotted past the car.

Glancing back, I saw a pair of Siamese cats drop out of an oak tree. They landed on the roof of the Lexus. Hopped down to the pavement. And joined the black cat, the tomcat, and a striped cat.

They're following me, I realized.

They're chasing me!

The cats broke into a run. I tore down the street and ran through the intersection.

I could see my house up ahead.

My legs pumped. Sweat dripped down my forehead. My heart thudded loudly.

I chanced one last glance over my shoulder.

There were at least ten cats now. Ten yowling cats, running hard.

Closing in.

Ten cats chasing me, eyes glowing, paws hitting the pavement so silently . . .

Silent as ghosts.

chapter

16

Could I outrun them?

I had to try.

They're only cats, I told myself.

Or *were* they?

Since when do cats travel in packs? And since when do cats chase after people?

My knee throbbed as I ran. My side ached.

I glanced back—and saw at least a dozen of them. Eyes glowing like fire. Paws pounding the sidewalk. Tails stiff and straight behind them.

"Ohhhhh." A low moan escaped my throat.

I gasped for breath. My driveway stood only a few yards away.

"Hey!" I cried out as I felt a claw dig into the back of my leg.

I turned and saw two cats leap at my back.

I ducked and they flew over my head.

Keeping low, my leg throbbing, I turned up the drive. Scrambled over the low rosebushes that lined the yard. And dove for the front stoop.

I grabbed the doorknob. Twisted it. Tugged.

"Ohhhh." Locked. Of course, it was locked.

I shoved my hand into my jeans pocket. Fumbled for the key.

Could I get inside before the cats attacked?

I pulled out the key—and dropped it. It clattered on the stoop and came to rest at the edge of the straw welcome mat.

"No!" I cried out. And bent to pick it up.

Turned to see if the cats were about to attack.

The cats . . .

No cats.

"Huh?" I swallowed hard.

They were gone. Vanished.

"H-how?" I choked out. But I didn't really care how they had disappeared so quickly. Or why they had appeared at all.

I just wanted to get inside. Inside, where I was safe.

I expected trouble over the rat incident. But nobody said a word about it.

Gayle passed me in the hall and didn't even glance my way.

Jessica also acted cold.

She must have heard about me and Kit, I figured. Probably from Riki.

But there wasn't much I could do about it.

I hoped Jessica wouldn't be too hurt. She seemed sweet. I liked her a lot—but Kit was awesome!

In one of my afternoon classes, Riki sneered at me. Then she raised her hand and made cat-clawing motions in the air.

Later I practiced with the team for the first time in a week. Barry, Dwayne, and I slipped back into our scoring routine as though I'd never been gone.

Kit and I studied math at my house until after nine that night. Before she left, we kissed again. And again.

The only time I didn't worry about what had been happening to me was when I spent time with Kit. She made everything okay.

The phone rang.

My eyes snapped open. I glanced at the clock next to my bed: 1:37 A.M.

Who could be calling at this hour?

I picked up the receiver. "Hello?" I said groggily.

Silence.

"Hell-oooo!" I sang, annoyed.

"Meow."

"Riki, cut it out," I snapped.

"Meowwwwww."

"Riki?" I asked.

Silence.

"Hey—who *is* this?" I cried angrily.

Another shrill cat hiss.

I hung up the phone.

The sound of the hiss lingered in my ears. I had to pull the covers up high to stop shivering.

chapter

17

My English class came right after lunch on my Friday schedule. That meant I spent half the class trying to stay awake, drowsy from having just eaten.

I sat in the back of the classroom and stared out at the dark clouds and the heavy rain, and wished for a couple of toothpicks to prop up my eyelids.

When the bell rang, I picked up my books and sleepwalked out into the hallway.

The biology lab was all the way on the other end of the school, and two floors down. I hurried along the hallway and tried to remember where I had stashed my bio homework.

I pushed through the stairwell door with a few dozen other kids, and started down.

"Hey, Marty," somebody called. "Good luck tonight."

At the landing between floors, the flow of students slipped around two people arguing angrily.

Dwayne and Riki.

Instead of calling out to them, I kept my mouth shut and followed the herd.

"What are you saying, Dwayne?" I heard Riki snap.

"Which word didn't you understand, Riki?" Dwayne replied nastily. "You're driving Marty nuts. It's time to drop all the cat nonsense. I want you to back off! Understand? Marty has to concentrate on basketball."

"Oh, I understand perfectly," Riki sneered as I slipped right by them. "You're threatening me now, right? What are you going to do if I don't leave Marty alone?"

"Tell the whole school we lost because of you," Dwayne announced.

I hurried past them. All through bio class, I thought about their argument.

I decided to have a talk with Dwayne. To tell him I could fight my own battles.

No matter how good a friend Dwayne was, I didn't want him speaking for me.

Riki didn't come to the game. I was glad.

But as the team jogged onto the court, I noticed Gayle sitting on the bleachers.

"What's she doing here?" I muttered to Barry, who ran next to me.

"Probably up there giving us the evil eye," he grumbled, shaking his head.

That game, Dwayne, Barry, and I played better together than ever before. The rest of the team kicked it into overdrive as well, and we destroyed the Truesdale Mustangs 67 to 42.

I don't think I'd ever been happier or more excited. The win gave us a slot in the state tournament.

I figured we couldn't lose. Not with *our* lineup. What I didn't know was that the lineup was about to change.

chapter

18

We had a wild celebration in the locker room. Then everybody left for home, totally psyched and ready for practice the next Monday.

As I drove away from school, I felt so excited, I could barely see straight.

I wondered if getting into the tournament would help me win my basketball scholarship. It better, I thought. That scholarship meant everything to me.

Of course, grades were important too.

Grades!

My books were in my backpack, which was either stashed in the locker room or somewhere in the gym.

"Man!" I scowled.

Then I did a U-turn in the middle of Division Street and drove back to the school.

When I turned into the student parking lot, all the lights had been turned out. I guessed even the maintenance staff had gone home.

My headlights washed over the back of the school. Something flashed in the lights.

The back door of the gym clanged off the brick wall.

Gayle's red hair flew behind her as she tore across the parking lot.

I watched her disappear into the darkness.

"Huh?" I murmured. "What is *she* doing here?"

I barely caught a glimpse of her face. But she seemed to be frantic. I wondered if she might be chasing somebody.

I stepped out of the car and searched for her. But it was too dark to see beyond the parking lot.

I jogged over to the door Gayle had left open. Good thing, I thought. Without the maintenance crew around to open the door, I would never have gotten back in.

I stepped into the dark hallway. One yellow light burned halfway between the exit door and the double doors to the gym.

My sneakers squeaked on the tile floor. The sound echoed in the empty hall.

The wind blew the door shut behind me—and I jumped.

"Whoa. Take it easy," I told myself out loud.

I stepped into the dark gym and shuffled to the

right. I ran my palm up and down the wall until, finally, I found a light switch.

I flipped it up.

Light flooded the gym.

I spotted my backpack at one corner of the street-side bleachers.

I sighed with relief and trotted over to get it.

As I bent to pick it up, I saw something under the bleachers.

A shoe?

No. I squinted harder. What was attached to the shoe?

A leg?

"Ohhhhh." A low moan escaped my throat. My backpack fell from my hands.

I crept over to the form. Dropped to my knees to see under the bleachers.

My hand sank into something wet. And sticky.

I jerked it up. Blood. Still warm.

A shudder swept down my body.

Without thinking, I wiped my hand on my jeans.

And gaped at the body sprawled under the bleachers.

Slashed and torn.

The face, the skin, clawed to pieces.

The shirt ripped and slashed. Covered with blood. Soaked with blood.

But I could still see that it was a Hawaiian shirt.

"Dwayne!"

Dwayne, lying dead and cut. Soaked in his own blood.

Slashed and torn.

"Nooooooooo," I wailed.

And over the sound of my cry, from the far bleachers, I heard the *meowwwwww* of a cat.

chapter

19

"Why didn't you tell the cops you saw Gayle there?" Barry asked angrily after the police had left my house.

"She didn't do it," I insisted.

The police questioned me at school first, then visited my house later that night. My mother had called Barry's mother and told her what had happened. Barry showed up while the police were still there, and they also questioned him.

I was afraid the police would think I killed Dwayne—because I had his blood on my clothes. But they didn't seem to suspect me.

When the police left, Barry and I didn't say anything to each other for a few minutes.

I couldn't even look at him.

No more Three Stooges. No more Three Musketeers. No more Hawaiian shirts. No more stupid
jokes.

No more Dwayne.

"So how do you know Gayle didn't do it?" Barry
argued. "She was the last one there, wasn't she?"

I sat on the couch in the living room, patting Teddy
on the head. Barry paced the rug.

"Gayle isn't a murderer," I said. "You know she
wouldn't kill anyone."

"Don't you ever watch the news, man?" Barry
cried. "That's what the friends and family of killers
always say! 'Oh, she seemed like such a nice girl!'
Wrong!"

"You didn't see Dwayne's body," I said quietly.
Calmly. "You didn't see what happened to him. Gayle
couldn't have done it. Do you understand me?"

Barry stared at his feet. "Man, I . . . I'm sorry," he
stammered. "I didn't think about what it was like for
you, finding him like that."

He lifted his eyes. "So who killed Dwayne if not
Gayle?" he asked.

I shrugged. I couldn't tell him about the cat I'd
heard just after I'd found Dwayne's body. About
everything that had happened to me since the cat in
the gym died.

Barry knew that something wasn't quite right. But
if I told him I thought a cat might have killed
Dwayne, he would have called me crazy.

* * *

"Oh, Marty, that's horrible," Kit groaned. "I'm so sorry. Is there anything I can do?"

"There isn't anything anybody can do," I answered, my voice cracking.

"Let me know if you need me," Kit said. "Call when you're ready—even if it's only to talk, okay?"

"Okay. Thanks. Thanks, Kit."

I had told Kit the bad news. Now I had one more chore to do.

I had to go see Gayle.

I rang her doorbell. Lights were on inside, but nobody appeared at the door.

I stepped off the porch and started to walk away. Then I heard a lock tumble open and the front door creak.

"Who's there?" a hoarse voice asked.

"Marty," I answered, stepping into the porch light.

"Oh, Marty!" Gayle sobbed. She threw open the door. There were tears on her face. What little make-up she wore had left a black trail on her cheeks.

"Gayle, I—" I began. But Gayle didn't listen. She threw her arms around me and hugged me tight.

"Marty, I'm so sorry about the horrible things I've done to you," she wailed.

"He's dead," she murmured. "I can't believe he's dead. I always liked Dwayne. In freshman year he was the only guy who noticed I even existed. He made me laugh so much. I feel as if I'll never laugh again!"

I wrapped my arms around Gayle. She'd been my worst enemy earlier in the day. But now I held her tight.

"It's okay," I whispered. "It's okay."

She pulled back again and wiped her eyes.

"What a jerk I am," she mumbled. "Your best friend is dead and I'm turning to you for a shoulder to cry on. I'm sorry, Marty."

"We can all cry together," another voice said.

Riki stepped into the hall, wiping the tears from her face.

I nodded to Riki. "You okay?"

"I guess."

"Gayle, there's something I want to ask you," I told her.

"Anything," she promised.

"I saw you running from the gym," I told her. "Just before I found Dwayne's body. What were you doing there?"

chapter

20

"Yes. I was there. And now I feel as if Dwayne's death is partly my fault," Gayle choked out.

"What do you mean?" I demanded.

"I hung around school after the game. The gymnastics coach said I could use the weight room. Then I realized how late it was. I had a baby-sitting job to get to. So I changed clothes in the locker room and ran out through the gym. If I hadn't been in such a rush, I might have seen the psycho who killed Dwayne," she explained.

She let out a sob. "But I was in such a hurry . . . oh, Marty, I'll do anything to help."

"Thanks, Gayle," I replied. "I'm not sure there's

anything anyone can do. But at least you've answered my question. I'll never doubt you again. I promise."

Dwayne was buried on Monday morning. Those of us who attended the funeral showed up late for school. The principal excused us all.

I could barely pay attention in class that afternoon. Later, as I trudged to basketball practice, I kept picturing Dwayne in his coffin.

I pushed open the door to the locker room. The rest of the team was already there.

Coach Griffin's eyes were red, as if he'd been crying. He handed a black armband to each of us.

"You don't have to wear these," he explained. "But I'm going to wear one at every practice, and at every tournament game, in memory of Dwayne."

All the guys slipped their armbands on.

But I only stared at the slender black-elastic cloth in my hands.

"Marty?" Coach asked.

"I don't know if I can play without him, Coach," I said in a whisper.

Coach Griffin didn't say anything for a minute. I expected him to urge me on, to tell me my feelings of loss would pass.

After all, Shadyside had never won the state tournament before, and Coach Griffin probably wanted that trophy more than anything.

"If you don't feel up to playing, Marty, we'll all understand," he said finally.

"I won't," Barry muttered.

"Excuse me?" I asked.

Barry sat on a bench across the room, his back against a row of gray metal lockers. "I said that I won't understand," he repeated, glaring at me.

Barry and I hadn't talked much after the night of Dwayne's death. I guess we were both so broken up that seeing each other would have been too painful.

"How could you even *think* about not playing?" Barry demanded. "Dwayne was my friend too, Marty. We were Three Musketeers, remember? Not two."

"I know," I admitted.

"I don't care if we win or lose," Barry declared. "But Dwayne would have wanted us to play."

I stared at my sneakers for a few seconds. Then I raised my eyes to meet Barry's.

"Playing isn't enough," I told him as I slipped on the armband. "We're going to win the tournament for Dwayne."

"For Dwayne!" the team echoed.

We never practiced so hard.

During practice, Riki sat high on the bleachers with Gayle and a few other girls. Barry and I waved to them, and they waved back. There were more kids than usual at practice. I chalked it up to excitement about the state tournament.

"You want to study together tonight?" Barry asked me in the locker room after practice.

"I have a six-to-nine shift at the animal shelter. Maybe I can come by after that," I suggested.

"Cool." He nodded. "Oh, hey—can you drop me off on the way home?"

"No problem," I agreed. "But hurry up, okay?"

I knew I would have to rush home and eat dinner quickly if I wanted to be on time for work. A few more shifts and my sentence would be completed. I couldn't wait.

I showered quickly and pulled on my clothes.

"Barry, hurry up, will you!" I called back into the showers.

"I'll be right out!" he promised.

"You leaving, Marty?" Kevin Hackett asked as he slung his backpack over his shoulder.

"Yeah," I answered. Then I called in to Barry, "I'll meet you at the back door!"

"Okay!"

Kevin and I pushed through the rear exit door.

We talked for a couple of minutes, mainly about classes. We were in the same history class, but he didn't seem any better prepared than I was.

A few teachers' cars were still parked in the faculty lot. A lot of them worked late, I noticed.

The side gym door hung open. The same door Gayle ran out of the night of Dwayne's murder.

As I thought about her, Gayle stepped through that door again. She glanced anxiously at her watch and tapped her foot. She didn't see me, and I didn't go over to her.

"What's holding Barry up?" I complained.

"There's my dad," Kevin announced. "Got to go." He hurried away.

As Kevin and his dad drove out, they passed a police car pulling in. It slid into a parking space and the engine cut off. The officer behind the wheel didn't get out. Instead, he sat and watched the parking lot. The police were watching the school after practice and at night. Obviously, they thought the murderer might return.

I chewed my lip nervously. And glanced at my watch.

"Come on, Barry," I muttered.

I pulled open the rear door and tromped back to the locker room.

"Let's go!" I called. "You're making me late!"

I didn't see Barry.

"Barry, come on!" I shouted. I stuck my head into the showers. No sign of him.

He wasn't in the locker room. "Oh, man," I whispered, shaking my head.

"Barry?"

No answer.

I shoved open the door to the gym. "Barry?" I called. Someone had turned out the lights. My voice echoed through the darkness.

Squinting hard, my eyes fell on a crumpled, still form at half court.

Oh, no . . . not again! my mind screamed. *"Nooooo!"*

chapter

21

My heart pounding, I stared at the un-
moving form on the wooden floor.

I blinked once. Twice. My eyes adjusted to the
shadowy light.

With a trembling hand I fumbled for the light
switch and flipped it on.

Barry's green backpack lay on the floor in the center
of the gym.

Not Barry.

Not Barry.

Barry's backpack.

I rushed across the gym to pick up the backpack. As
I bent down, I heard voices from outside the gym
doors. I hurried over to the double doors, which were
open slightly.

"Barry?" I called as I pushed open a door.

In the hall, Barry stood with his arms wrapped around Riki. They were kissing. But they pulled apart quickly when they saw me.

"Oh! Hey, Marty," Barry fumbled.

Riki smiled. "Hi, Marty."

"Hey, guys," I answered.

So, Barry and Riki were together. It was cool with me. Barry needed a girlfriend. And I'd made it clear that I wasn't interested in Riki.

I grinned at Riki. "Now I know why Gayle is hanging around outside, staring at her watch."

"Whoops!" Riki giggled. "I hope she isn't too steamed. I . . . uh . . . I got hung up." She smiled at Barry.

"Listen, Barry, I really have to go. I'm definitely going to be late for work," I explained. "Sorry I can't wait."

"That's okay," he answered. "No problem. Maybe Gayle will drop me off."

I slid Barry's backpack over to him.

"See you later?" Barry asked.

"I'll do my best," I promised.

"You're late, Marty," my boss scolded me.

"Sorry, Carolyn. I don't really have a good excuse," I admitted.

"I'll forgive you this time. How are you doing?" she asked, her expression softening. Her eyes studied me.

"I'm dealing with things," I told her. "Sometimes I

just can't believe Dwayne is dead—you know? I can't imagine what it will be like to never see him again."

Carolyn laid a hand on my shoulder. "It's tough. Glad you're handling it."

She sighed. "I wish I could stay and talk, Marty. But I have to get going. First, though, you should meet our new inmate, Brutus."

"Brutus?"

She led me into the kennel area.

"I dug through the basement storage for this cage today," Carolyn explained.

I stared at Brutus. Much larger than any of the others, his cage stood at the end of the row.

"Wow!" I cried, moving closer to the huge animal. "I didn't know you sheltered *werewolves* here!"

Carolyn didn't laugh at my joke.

"Keep your distance, Marty," she warned. "Brutus is dangerous. The vet is coming here in the morning to put him to sleep."

I stared at the huge mongrel dog. It must have weighed two hundred pounds!

It didn't bark or growl at me. But I hung back.

When I was a kid, my dad explained to me that quiet dogs were sometimes more dangerous because you didn't know what to expect.

After Carolyn left, I fed all the dogs and cats. Brutus shifted uneasily when I slipped his food dish in the cage. He lowered his head and stared at me with yellow eyes.

A few cats paced their cages nervously. But the big kennel room was quiet.

I pulled a broom from the supply closet and started to sweep. I was in the middle of the room—in the aisle between the cats and dogs—when I heard a sound.

A soft, scraping sound.

A footstep.

I leaned on the broom and listened. My mouth suddenly felt dry. My legs were trembling.

Another footstep.

I gripped the broom handle so hard, my hands ached.

"Who—who's there?" I choked out.

No answer.

"Hey—who's there?" I shouted.

I heard another footstep. From the far wall.

And then a clank. The clank of metal.

A dog barked. Then another. It started them all barking.

I raised the broom, as if to use it as a weapon. I took a step toward the sounds.

The cats began to yowl.

Over the noise I heard another metallic clang.

A cage door slamming against a cage.

The cats hissed and yowled. Dogs barked.

"Hey!" I shouted.

A cat stepped into the aisle.

"Huh?" I let out a startled gasp.

Another cat stepped up beside it.

I heard another cage door clang open.

Two more cats leapt into the aisle. They arched

98

their backs. Their teeth shone in the light as they hissed at me.

I took a step back. "What's going on?" I cried.

Why was someone opening the cage doors? Who was in here?

"Please—" I started to say.

Another cage door clanged open. More cats jammed the aisle.

Dogs barked and howled.

A yellow cat dove for me. It raised a front paw and clawed the air.

"Noooo!" I shrank back.

I heard another loud clang. Closer.

But I couldn't see anyone.

The cats edged closer, clawing the air. Hissing. Their tails straight up. Backs arched.

"Who is here? Who is doing this?" I shrieked.

The cats moved faster now. Their eyes glowed. Threatening eyes. Cold eyes.

I backed up. One step. Then another.

The hissing and yowling sounds were deafening. But I couldn't pay attention.

The cats were forming a circle. Surrounding me.

They arched up on their hind legs. A dozen hissing cats. They bared their teeth. Raised their claws.

And leapt to the attack.

chapter

22

"N<small>OOOOOOO</small>!"

A hoarse wail escaped my throat. I raised the broom between my hands.

Two shrieking cats jumped for my chest.

I caught them with the broom handle—and sent them flying over the cages.

"Marty—what are you DOING?"

A voice rang out over the barking and shrieking of the animals.

I staggered back until I hit the wall.

The cats slunk back. They were silent now. Staring up at me with their glowing eyes.

The dogs stopped barking.

Feeling dazed, I struggled to catch my breath. Sweat ran down my forehead. My whole body trembled.

Carolyn stepped into the aisle, her eyes wild with shock. "Marty—why?"

The broom fell from my hands.

Carolyn picked up a black cat and gently placed it in a cage. The cats were all purring softly now.

"S-somebody was here!" I gasped, swallowing hard. "Somebody let them out."

Carolyn turned and searched the room. "Who was here?" She turned back to me, her face filled with concern. "Marty, the door is locked. No one could get in."

"No. Really—" I insisted, my heart still pounding.

Carolyn rounded up more cats and returned them to their cages. I didn't move from the wall. My legs were still trembling too hard to walk.

"They . . . attacked me!" I told her. "Someone opened the cages and—"

"Marty, let's go to the office," Carolyn said sternly. She motioned with her hand. "Please. Go in and sit down."

I obediently left the kennel and made my way to the office. On the way, I took a drink of water from the fountain.

If only I could stop shaking!

Carolyn joined me in the office a few minutes later. She was chewing her bottom lip and eyeing me thoughtfully as she took a seat behind her desk.

"Carolyn—" I began.

But she raised a hand to silence me. "Marty, I know you've been through a shock," she said softly. "But you have to realize—*you* opened those cages. *You* let those cats out."

"No—" I insisted. "Listen to me—"

She shook her head. "There is no one else in here, Marty. You were alone with the animals. Alone. I came back because I forgot my purse. And there you were. The cages open. The cats all over the floor."

"But—they *attacked* me!" I cried.

She shook her head again. She raised a finger to her lips. "I saw *you* attacking them," she said. "I saw you swing the broom. The cats were just watching you."

"No!" I cried. "You've *got* to believe me!"

"I believe that you're stressed. And horribly upset. And maybe in shock," Carolyn replied. "I'm going to drive you home, Marty. And I want you to talk to your parents. Maybe see a doctor. And take some time to get yourself together."

She stood up and came around to my chair. "I'm worried about you. I really am."

I was worried about me too.

Could Carolyn be right? Was I really in shock?

Did I let those cats out of their cages?

No. No way, I told myself.

But could I be sure?

"I—I can drive myself home," I told her. I stood up shakily. "I'm really sorry," I murmured. "I—I still have five hours to serve. Do you want—"

"I want you to come back when you feel you are ready," she said. "Sure you don't want me to drive you?"

"No. Thanks. My car is right outside."

She kept her hand on my shoulder as I led the way to the door. Then she stood in the doorway, watching me as I backed the car up and pulled away.

"Wow," I said aloud, turning toward Fear Street. "Wow. Wow."

I still felt shaky. I didn't want to go home. I didn't want to tell Mom and Dad what had happened. But I needed to talk to someone.

So I drove to Barry's.

The house was completely dark as I pulled up the driveway. That's weird, I thought. He knew I planned to come over after work.

He must be in the back, I decided.

I climbed out of the car—and tripped over his little brother's tricycle. "Owww!" I toppled to the asphalt. Skinned my hand.

"Bad night," I muttered. I pulled myself up, brushed myself off, and made my way to the front door.

"Hey—" To my surprise, the door was open a few inches.

Someone is getting careless, I thought.

I pushed the door open a little wider and peered into the living room. Completely dark.

"Anybody home?" I called in. "Hey, Barry—you home?"

No reply.

I took a step into the room. "Barry? You here? It's me."

Silence.

"Hey—you left your door open!" I shouted.

Still no reply. So I decided to try the back of the house.

I took a few steps toward the hall—and tripped over something soft and heavy on the living room floor.

chapter
23

"Oh, no!"

A cry escaped my throat.

I dropped to my knees. "Barry? Barry?"

With a hoarse cry, I reached up—and clicked on a table lamp.

And stared at what I had tripped over.

A rolled-up carpet.

I uttered a long sigh. "Marty, you're losing it," I told myself. "You're totally losing it."

"Hey—is somebody there?" I heard Barry call from the back of the house.

I jumped up. I heard whispering. Then a girl's giggle.

"It's me," I called. Stepping over the carpet, I hurried into the den.

And found Barry and Riki sitting close—very close—together on the leather couch.

Barry had dark red lipstick smears on his cheek. Riki's hair was wild around her face. Barry's arm was wrapped around her shoulders.

"Hey—hi!" Barry greeted me with a grin. "What's up, Marty? We were . . . uh . . ."

Riki slid away from him. She pushed back her hair with both hands.

"The door was open," I said, pointing awkwardly. "I didn't mean to—"

"I thought you were working at the shelter tonight," Riki said, straightening her sweater. "Barry said you were coming over later."

"I—I had to leave early," I stammered. "You see, a really weird thing happened. And Carolyn thought I should go home and—"

"Who's Carolyn?" Riki asked.

"She's my boss there," I explained. "You see, somebody let the cats out of the cages. And—"

"Excuse me?" Barry interrupted.

"The cats all got out," I repeated urgently. "And they attacked me. They backed me against a wall. And if Carolyn hadn't forgotten her purse . . ."

My voice trailed off. I saw the way they were staring at me.

They didn't believe me. And why should they?

I wasn't making any sense.

The whole story didn't make any sense.

They didn't believe me—and they didn't want to

hear a wild story about cages that opened by themselves and cats that attacked humans. They wanted to be alone so they could make out.

I could see all that on their faces.

Barry uttered a sigh. "Maybe I could call you later?" he suggested. He kept giving me eye signals.

"Yeah. Okay." I could take a hint.

"Are you okay, Marty?" Riki asked. "You look kind of . . . messed up."

"No. I'll be okay," I murmured. "Later, guys." I turned and hurried out of the den. I ran across the dark living room, nearly tripping over the rolled-up carpet again.

"Whoa!" I let out a cry. Hopped over it. Burst out of the house at a run.

And bumped into a large, gray-haired man coming up the walk.

We both let out cries of surprise.

"Who are you?" the man demanded. He narrowed his eyes at me. Studied me.

"I'm Barry's friend," I replied breathlessly.

He nodded, keeping his eyes on me. "I'm a neighbor," he said, motioning to the house across the driveway. "I saw the front door open over here. I was just coming over to make sure everything is okay."

"Yeah. It's fine," I told him. "I think Barry just forgot to close it all the way."

The neighbor studied me some more. Then he grunted and turned to go back to his house. "Nice night," he murmured as he walked away.

"Not really," I replied softly.

Not a nice night at all, I decided. In fact, one of the most frightening nights of my life.

I had no idea that the frights had just begun.

*T*he next morning, my mother knocked on my bedroom door at a little after seven o'clock. Heavy rain pounded my windows and gray clouds blotted out the sun.

I wanted to pull the pillow over my head and keep sleeping. I'd hit the snooze button twice already though. Once more, and I would definitely be late for school.

"Marty? Are you awake?" Mom called from the hallway.

"Yeah!" I groaned. "I'm up. I'll be down in a few."

"Can I come in?" she asked.

"Sure," I answered.

When she opened the door, I could see that she'd been crying. Her eyes were red and puffy. She ran a hand through her hair and said, "Put something on and hurry downstairs, Marty."

"What is it, Mom?" I asked. "What's happened?"

"Marty," Mom whispered, wiping a tear from her cheek. "Marty, there are police officers downstairs who need to speak with you."

My heart sank. Police officers.

I pulled on a pair of jeans and a sweatshirt. Then I followed my mother down the stairs.

Why was my mother crying? The question haunted me as I stepped into the living room. Two uniformed police officers stood close together, whispering.

"Officer Martinez, Officer Lambert, this is my son, Marty," Mom told them.

"Hi," I mumbled.

"Marty, please have a seat," Office Martinez suggested. It bothered me that he offered me a seat in my own house.

I sat down and waited. The police didn't say anything for a few seconds.

"Is this about last night?" I asked, sick of waiting.

"What about last night?" Officer Lambert inquired, and narrowed his eyes.

"At the animal shelter," I explained. "Someone opened the cages and—"

The cops glanced at each other, then at my mother. Finally, they turned their attention back to me.

"No. It's not about the shelter," Officer Lambert said.

"Marty, did you go anywhere after you left the animal shelter last night?" Martinez asked.

"Sure." I shrugged. "I went to my friend Barry's house. We were supposed to study. But his girlfriend was there, so I left."

"His girlfriend?" Lambert asked. "That would be Riki Crawford?"

"Yeah," I agreed. "Look, did something happen at the shelter after I left? Is Carolyn okay?"

"She is fine, Marty," Officer Martinez assured me.

Then my heart nearly stopped.

"Oh, no," I whispered. "Please don't tell me something's happened to Barry. Please—"

The cops lowered their eyes. Lambert bit his lip before speaking.

"I'm sorry, Marty," he said softly. "Someone murdered your friend Barry last night. He was clawed to pieces."

chapter

25

"**D**wayne and Barry," I whispered. "Dwayne and Barry. It's *impossible.*"

"Oh, Marty, it's so awful," my mom sobbed. She shook her head, her chin quivering. "I'm so sorry."

She wrapped her arms around me.

I sat in the chair and stared at nothing. I couldn't hug her back.

I couldn't even cry.

"Marty? Do you need a few minutes?" Officer Martinez asked. "I could go and come back."

The police officer's question snapped me out of the trance I'd slipped into.

"No. No, I'll be okay, I guess," I mumbled. "What did you want to know?"

My mom walked around the front of the couch and

sat down next to me. The police officers still didn't sit, and it made me nervous.

As if they were vultures, staring down at me.

"Perhaps you want a lawyer present?" Officer Martinez asked. "We have to give you that choice."

I shook my head. "I'll answer your questions. I want to help."

"What time did you leave Barry's house last night, Marty?" Lambert asked.

"I don't know." I shrugged. "A little before ten, I think. Riki might remember better. She was still there with him when I left."

"A neighbor saw you run from the house," Lambert said, his eyes burning into mine. "The neighbor said you looked wild, very excited."

"Wait a minute!" I cried. "You guys don't think I killed him? You've got to be out of your minds!"

The officers both raised their eyebrows.

Then Martinez shrugged. "Look at it from our point of view, Marty," he began. "We've been aware of every incident in which you were involved over the past few weeks."

"Huh?" I cried. "Incident?"

He nodded. "First, there was the killing of the cat in the high school gym. Then you behaved strangely at the Student Court session. You told everyone that you saw a dead cat where there was nothing at all. Then you were the one to discover Dwayne Clark's body."

I felt sick. I couldn't argue with anything he said.

"Finally, last night at the animal shelter," the officer continued, "the manager told us she found the cats all loose. And you were batting at them with a broom."

"This is insane!" my mom burst out. "Dwayne and Barry were my son's best friends!"

"I'm not a killer!" I cried. "Okay. Okay. I killed the cat. But it was an accident. I would never hurt anyone. Especially not my best friends."

Martinez motioned with both hands for me to calm down.

"Sorry," I muttered. "I—I'm so upset. I don't know what to say. You don't *really* think I killed Barry, do you?"

"Not really," Martinez replied. "But we have to follow up on every lead. Riki Crawford told us that you left the house before she did. She left at eleven, and called Barry as soon as she got home. He was still okay at eleven-thirty."

"That gives you an alibi," his partner said.

"It gives her an alibi too," Martinez added.

The officers rose to leave. Then Martinez grabbed Lambert's arm, and they turned to face me.

"One more question," Officer Martinez began. "Didn't you say the Allens' door was open when you arrived?"

"Yes," I replied.

"Your friend Riki remembered you saying something about the door being open," Martinez continued. "But she swears that when she and Barry sat down in the den, the front door was closed and locked."

"What do you mean?" I demanded, feeling very confused.

"Are you saying the killer might already have been inside the house when Marty got there?" my mother asked.

The officers nodded. I watched them walk to the door. I didn't show them out. I could barely move a muscle.

Of course school was canceled. Miss Bevan, the vice principal, called Mom and said that special counselors were being called in to talk to students about the two murders.

Mom said that I should go and talk with them. But I really didn't feel like talking to anyone.

What was there to say?

I stayed in my room all morning, feeling totally numb. I couldn't think. I couldn't cry. I couldn't do anything at all.

A little after noon, I went downstairs and made myself a sandwich. I took one bite and couldn't finish the rest.

I sat in the kitchen staring at it for a while. Then I picked up the phone and called Kit.

"Marty, how are you doing?" she asked.

"I—I don't know. I think I'm in shock or something. I can't think straight."

"I'm in shock too," Kit replied. "I just can't believe it."

We were both silent for a while. I could hear her breathing.

"They said on the news that Barry was clawed to death," Kit said finally. "It—it's just so unbelievable, Marty." Her voice broke.

"Yeah." I sighed. "Unbelievable."

"Both guys—kids we *know*—clawed to death. Is the killer *crazy?* He's like a vicious animal!"

I didn't reply. I suddenly wanted to get off the phone. I couldn't talk about it. Why had I called Kit?

"Riki was there with Barry last night?" Kit asked. "I heard that she—"

"Yeah. She was with him," I interrupted. "But she says she left at eleven and talked with him later."

"She must be really messed up," Kit said. "Maybe I'll give her a call."

"That would be nice," I replied.

"We all just have to be nice to each other," Kit said. "And maybe we'll get through it."

"Maybe," I replied, feeling my throat tighten. "I—I just can't believe it all started with a stupid cat."

"You don't really believe—" Kit started to say.

But I couldn't talk anymore. I could feel myself breaking down. "Later, Kit," I choked out. I hung up before she could say anything else.

I don't know *what* I did the rest of the afternoon. I really don't remember.

The next day, the school held a special assembly for Dwayne and Barry.

It was very sad. Just about everyone cried.

The grief counselors offered to meet with any students who wanted their help.

Afterward, Coach Griffin held a team meeting. It was the quietest meeting we ever had.

"How do you boys feel?" Coach asked. "Feel like playing in the tournament? Or should we give it a miss? Be honest. I'll do whatever you say."

All eyes turned to me.

Everyone knew that Dwayne and Barry had been my best friends.

"We—we can't win without them," I murmured. "I don't think we should play."

A few guys nodded. But others protested.

Kevin spoke up. "Marty, after Dwayne's death you were the one who said we should play for him. Now I think we should play our best—and play for Dwayne and Barry."

We talked about it a little while longer. Then we voted to continue in the tournament.

I pictured my two friends dribbling down the court, teasing each other, heaving up long, graceful layups.

I had to get out of that gym. Away from everyone.

I burst out the door, into the hall, and jogged to my locker.

Two girls were huddled against the wall, both talking at once. Gayle and Riki. They stopped talking when they saw me approach.

Riki rushed up and gave me a hug. "How's it going?" she whispered.

I shrugged. "You know."

They exchanged glances.

They both appeared really tense.

"What's going on?" I murmured. "You stopped talking when I showed up."

"We were . . . uh . . . talking about you," Riki replied, her eyes on Gayle.

"Marty, we're kind of worried," Gayle said. "I mean, about you."

"Me?" I narrowed my eyes at them. "I'm handling it," I said. "I guess."

"No. That's not what we mean," Riki chimed in. "We mean . . . Dwayne . . . Barry . . . you guys were the Three Musketeers—right?"

I nodded.

"And someone murdered them. And now there's only one left. You."

I finally caught on to what they were saying. I'd been thinking so much about my two dead friends, it never crossed my mind.

"You mean?"

Gayle's eyes burned into mine. "Do you think you could be *next?*" she asked.

chapter

26

When I showed up at the animal shelter a few nights later, Carolyn greeted me with surprise. "Marty—how are you doing?" she asked, her eyes studying me closely.

"Okay, I guess," I told her. "It's been rough. But I'm trying to keep it together."

"You really didn't need to come tonight," she said. "If you want to wait a few weeks . . ."

"No. I need to keep busy," I told her. "You know. Keep my mind off things."

She led me to the kennel area. "I've already fed them all," she said. "I didn't think you were coming. So I guess you can just sweep and clean up."

A loud bark made me spin around. "Hey!" I cried.

"That mean dog—Brutus. I thought he was being put down."

"He got a last-minute rescue," Carolyn replied. "We may have an owner for Brutus. Someone who is looking for a really frightening dog to guard his store."

"Brutus got a job," I muttered. The dog growled at me.

"I think it's a bad idea," Carolyn said. "Brutus is really bad tempered. But—"

The phone rang. Carolyn hurried to the office to answer it.

I made my way through the aisle between the cages to the supply closet. "Hope you guys are going to behave tonight," I told the cats.

A few minutes later, Carolyn said good night. I heard the front door close behind her. Then I heard her car pull out of the parking lot.

I leaned against the broom, shoving it along the first aisle. Being back there in the shelter gave me the creeps. But I only had a few more hours to serve.

And I was desperate to keep busy. Desperate to keep my mind busy.

If only it would stay quiet in here tonight, I hoped.

I didn't get my wish.

I was sweeping the last aisle when the cats began to hiss.

A few cats at first. At the other side of the kennel.

But the sound quickly swept through the room, like a strong, angry wind.

"Stop it!" I shouted. "Stop it right now!"

I know it was stupid. Shouting at cats.

And it only seemed to get them more excited.

I let go of the broom and covered my ears. Cats yowled and hissed. The deafening noise made the dogs start to bark.

"Is someone here?" I called.

Was someone causing the animals to go nuts?

"Is someone here?" I shouted at the top of my voice.

No reply.

Dogs bumped the sides of their cages as if trying to break out. Cats arched their backs and hissed.

I'm just going to leave, I decided.

There's no reason to stay here.

I turned toward the office—and gasped in shock.

"Kit!" I cried.

She stepped out from behind a row of cat cages. She had a big gray sweatshirt pulled down over black tights. Her hair hung loosely around her face.

"Kit—" I shouted over the animal cries and hisses. "What are you doing here? I'm so glad to see you!"

To my surprise, her expression turned hard and cold. "It's your turn, Marty," she said.

chapter

28

"Huh?" I took a few steps toward her. "Kit—what did you say? It's so noisy in here."

She raised one hand.

The hissing and barking stopped.

"Hey—magic!" I cried. "What's going on here?"

"It's your turn, Marty," she repeated, her eyes staring into mine, cold as ice.

"My turn? I don't understand."

"You killed me," she said in a low, even tone. "You killed me, and then your two friends laughed."

I stepped up to her, my mind spinning. "Kit—are you okay?" I asked. "You're not making any sense."

Her expression grew even colder. She pulled back her lips and uttered a frightening hiss. "I'm the cat,

Marty," she whispered. "I'm the stray. The cat from the gym. The cat you and your friends killed."

"Whoa!" I cried. "Calm down. Just calm down."

I put my hands on her shoulders. But she let out another animal hiss and jerked away from me.

Her face filled with hatred. Her green eyes flared angrily.

"Calm down," I repeated. "I'll get you to a doctor. You'll be okay. It's the strain, Kit. It's all the horror of the past week. It's making you say crazy things. But . . . I'll get you help."

"I'm the cat, Marty," she repeated. "You met my family—remember? The other cats in my house? Those are my brothers and sisters."

"But, Kit—" I started to say.

She raised a hand and clawed the air.

"I'm a shape-shifter," she continued. "I'm one of the last shape-shifters on earth. I shift between a girl and a cat. It's so easy for me."

She took a step closer. "Why did you kill me, Marty? Why did you do it? Why were you and your friends always so eager to get rid of me?"

"Kit, please—" I begged. "You're not a cat. You're just very mixed up right now. But you'll be okay. I promise."

"Do you know why I hung around in the gym?" she demanded. "Do you know why I lived under the bleachers? To be close to you!"

"Huh?" I gasped.

"I stayed there to watch you," she insisted. "That's how crazy I was about you."

She sneered. "That's true love, Marty. And how did you pay me back? You dropped me off the bleachers. You tried to kill me. You didn't know that I'm blessed with nine lives."

I stared hard at her. My mouth had dropped open. I didn't believe any of it. Not a word.

It was all totally crazy. Poor Kit had freaked out.

"I'll get you help," I told her.

"No, you won't," she shot back. "You're dead, Marty. I'll miss you. I really will. But I've been playing with you too long. It's time to finish this."

"Listen to me—" I tried to explain.

But I stopped when I saw her start to change.

Gray fur sprouted quickly over her face. Her features melted together as whiskers poked out from under her nose.

She slid out from her clothes, covered in gray fur now. Shrinking . . . shrinking . . .

Down on all fours. Her hands and feet turning into paws. A tail rising stiffly behind her. Her lips pulled back in a shrill cat hiss.

"Noooooooo!" A wail of horror, of total disbelief, escaped my throat.

I was staring at the cat. The gray cat with the black diamond forehead.

I was staring at Kit. Staring at the cat.

Staring at the cat I had killed.

"No—please!" I begged.

I staggered back.

Not fast enough.

She leapt high, raising two sharp-clawed paws.

I felt a sharp stab of pain run over my face.

Saw bright red blood—*my* blood!—spatter to the floor.

"Ohhhhhh." The pain shot down my entire body.

She pulled away her claws. I saw chunks of my skin in them.

Holding my bleeding face, I dropped to my knees. And saw her raise her claws to slash again.

chapter

29

"OWWWWWW!"

I let out a shriek as the cat's claws cut through my shirt, tearing open my skin.

Kit screeched. Her eyes danced happily.

She leapt again.

I dodged away. She landed hard beside me on the kennel floor.

The pain shot through my body, doubling me over. My blood spattered the floor.

Lifting my head, I saw her raise herself. Prepare to attack again.

I groaned.

No way to escape.

She's going to kill me, I realized. She's going to slash me to pieces.

She tossed back her head in a shrill screech. And dove at me again.

I turned—and her claws scraped my side.

Everything went red. Red as my blood.

I choked. Gasped for breath.

I felt myself going under. Fading . . . fading into the red.

"Nooo!" I moaned. I pushed myself forward. Grabbed the dog cages for support.

Heaved myself away from her.

A sharp growl made me stop.

Through the pain, through the billowing red, I gazed down. Brutus.

The big dog growled up at me.

I heard Kit screech. Turned and saw her running toward me on all fours. Eyes wild. Fur standing on end as if electric.

"Brutus," I groaned.

I fumbled with the latch. My hand trembling so bad, I couldn't work it.

Finally I jerked open the cage door.

The big dog lumbered out just as Kit attacked.

I collapsed to the floor. The pain swept over me. Pulled me down . . . down.

But I raised my head in time to see the big dog clamp its jaws around the cat.

Kit shrieked and clawed.

I heard a sickening *crack* as Brutus snapped her neck between his teeth.

Kit let out a long, breathy wheeze. Her body slumped lifelessly in the dog's jaws.

And I sank to the floor. And watched the curtain of red darken to black.

CRT

At last a dog, Looking relieved that they
stopped listening to the dog's cries.

And I sank to the floor, and wept on the bottom of
the animal shelter.

chapter
30

*T*he emergency room doctor shook his head. He had stitched me up and checked me out.

"I still don't believe it," he murmured. "A *cat* did that to you?"

I nodded grimly. "Yeah. A cat. I don't know why it attacked me. But I'm never going back to that animal shelter. I can promise you that."

"I think that's smart," the doctor agreed. "I don't think you and animals get along."

What an understatement! I thought.

As I left the hospital with my parents, I wished I could tell them the truth.

But there was no way they would ever believe me.

My parents don't believe in shape-shifters. I don't know *anyone* who believes in shape-shifters.

Except for me, of course.

Riki called a few hours after I got home. I was so sore, I could barely hold the phone to my ear. But we had a nice talk.

She's really okay, I decided. In fact, she's terrific.

I decided to apologize to her for the way I had treated her before. Maybe she and I could try again—now that all the horror was over.

The first basketball tournament game was the next Friday night. I still felt sore, and my side throbbed every time I caught the ball. But I was so happy to be back on the court, so happy to be having a normal life again, I ignored the pain and played my hardest.

With less than two minutes in the game, we were down by one basket.

A three-point shot would move us ahead. And then maybe we could hang on to win.

Kevin and Joe Gimmell passed the ball back and forth as they thundered down the court. I trotted near the foul line, trying to get open.

I faked left. Joe could see that I was open.

"Pass it! Pass it!" I shouted.

He stopped dribbling and raised the ball as if he were going for the three-pointer himself.

Then he heaved the ball to me.

I reached for it.

And saw a green glow under the bleachers.

Two green glows.

Two green eyes. Of a cat.

131

A gray cat with a black diamond on its forehead.
The ball bounced off my chest.
The crowd groaned.
I didn't care.
I stared at the cat. She raised blood-smeared claws.
And I started to scream.

About the Author

"Where do you get your ideas?"

That's the question that R. L. Stine is asked most often. "I don't know where my ideas come from," he says. "But I do know that I have a lot more scary stories in my mind that I can't wait to write."

So far, he has written over a hundred mysteries and thrillers for young people, all of them bestsellers.

Bob grew up in Columbus, Ohio. Today he lives in an apartment near Central Park in New York City with his wife, Jane, and son, Matt.

THE NIGHTMARES
NEVER END . . .
WHEN YOU VISIT

Next . . .
HIGH TIDE
(Coming mid-May 1997)

Adam Malfitano still has nightmares about the night his girlfriend, Mitzi, died. He sees the blood. He sees her in the water. He is a lifeguard and he can't save her. He wakes up screaming.

Even worse, he has begun to see Mitzi while he is *awake*. He knows it is impossible . . . but she looks so real. He can see her face decaying. What does she want from him? Why won't she leave him alone? He tried to save her—doesn't she know that?

R.L. STINE'S GHOSTS OF FEAR STREET ®

Simon & Schuster Mail Order
200 Old Tappan Rd., Old Tappan, N.J. 07675
Please send me the books I have checked above. I am enclosing $_____ (please add
$0.75 to cover the postage and handling for each order. Please add appropriate sales
tax). Send check or money order--no cash or C.O.D.'s please. Allow up to six weeks
for delivery. For purchase over $10.00 you may use VISA: card number, expiration
date and customer signature must be included.

POCKET
BOOKS

Name _____

Address _____

City _____ State/Zip _____

VISA Card # _____ Exp.Date _____

Signature _____ 1180-16